EMBRACED

JUS ACCARDO

Entangled Publishing, LLC
2614 South Timberline Road
Suite 109
Fort Collins, CO 80525
Visit our website at www.entangledpublishing.com.

Embrace is an imprint of Entangled Publishing, LLC.

Edited by Liz Pelletier
Cover design by Heather Howland
Cover art from iStock

Manufactured in the United States of America

First Edition November 2015

embrace

This book is for Liz, Nicole, Heather, Melanie, and Jessica. Again, thank you doesn't cover it.

Chapter One

This sucked.

Bodies grinding against each other on the dance floor. Crowding around the bars. They were even lined up two deep against the walls, several locked at the lips and going at it like crazed fucking rabbits. The whole club reeked of lust. The orange mist it gave off bled into the air and swirled around like smog, mingling with the always present taint of red. Anger. You couldn't have one without the other. It made the world go round.

It made *my* world go round…

I inhaled, taking it all in. Azirak—Azi—the demon royal that had lived inside me my entire life, nibbled at the emotion and rumbled with contentment. That was a demon for you. Always getting off on the dark side of humanity. It needed them to survive. Since we were shacked up in the same space—I was a descendant of Cain, born with a demon fused to my soul—in a twisted way I needed them, too.

A few feet away, a guy let out a yell and threw his bottle of Bud on the ground. It shattered, splattering liquid and glass everywhere as the surrounding crowd scattered and howled with laughter.

Fucking idiots.

The one plus to taking this job as a bouncer at The Viking? It was the perfect way to feed the demon's need for violence.

"Hey!" The guy heard me, but chose to ignore it, turning back to the girl he was with. Big mistake. I wove through the crowd, itching to introduce him to one — or both — of my fists. The last few nights had been slow. Other than taking harmless crumbs of anger and lust, Azi hadn't truly fed in over two days. I was starting to feel edgy. Fingers crossed this bastard started something. A good skull cracking would take the edge off. "Knock it the fuck off," I demanded, grabbing the back of his shirt and spinning him around to face me.

He immediately threw his hands up in surrender. The whole exchange was hardly worth my trouble.

Much to the demon's irritation, I let go of the guy and went back to tracking my original prey. He was tall, with dark hair and a stocky build, and had been following the same girl all night long — a small-framed brunette behind the bar on the other side of the club, serving drinks and seeming oblivious to his attention.

After a quick glance over his shoulder, the guy made his move. I started forward as the demon gave an uneasy rumble. Tall-dark-and-stalkery elbowed his way to the bar, leaning in to get the girl's attention. I had no idea what he'd said, but she looked confused.

"Blow him off, Sammy," I growled. "Stay behind the fucking bar." I was still cutting a path through the crowded club floor. When people didn't move out of the way fast enough, I started pushing.

The guy waved his arms and pointed to the back of the

club. After a minute of this, Sam shook her head and came around to his side of the bar. She called something to the other bartender and followed the guy into the crowd.

"Really?" I spat, willing her to feel my anger through our unwanted—and apparently useless—mental link. Nothing happened. Within seconds Sam's head disappeared, swallowed by a horde of drunk idiots.

I picked up the pace, roughly shoving away anyone in my path. When I reached the edge of the dance floor, she was just rounding the corner of the basement stairwell. I made it to the door in less than ten steps.

"I dunno what you heard, but I'm not into the whole three-way thing," I heard Sam say. She forced a laugh. "I'm betting you could find a more than willing participant upstairs, though. Try the bathroom by the door. Lots of weirdos hang out in there."

I eased the door closed so it didn't make any noise, then crept down the steps. Sam was at the bottom, by the spare bottles of liquor, and she wasn't alone. The guy from the bar was in front of her, and to his right was a tall woman with bright red hair. "Your bravado is unimpressive," she said. "You're going to come with us."

"That's really *not* gonna happen," Sam insisted, inching a hair to the left.

Azi flashed a series of images—the demon's primary means of communication—all involving the brutal beat down of the two intruders. Despite the wave of involuntary contentment at the scenario of massive carnage and snapping bones in my grasp, I tamped the urges down and stepped onto the landing.

"Will you submit to me?" he asked.

"Submit to you?" Sam repeated. There was the smallest warble in her voice. "What the hell is that supposed to mean?"

"Give yourself to us willingly. You'll feel no pain. I

promise." The guy stepped closer, and the moment he reached out to touch her, I propelled myself forward.

Azi roared, a jarring sound that rattled my entire body. The demon didn't push for control, but stayed close to the surface in case I needed it. I wouldn't. "I suggest you take the lady's advice and go find a different playmate."

The guy glared from Sam to me, then glanced at the red haired woman. She let out a horrible shriek and flung herself at me. As murderous as the urges the demon spurred in me, I refused to hit a woman. Human, at least. But that didn't stop me from raising my arm to protect myself.

It wasn't my fault she knocked herself out on my elbow.

"See, Sammy?" I said, straightening. I rolled up the sleeve of my black *Viking Security* T-shirt and flexed. In the short time I'd been working as a bouncer at Harlow's one and only nightclub, I'd developed a wicked reputation. "Told you my biceps were dangerous."

"Leave," the guy commanded. With impressive speed for a human, he moved in to wrap his hand around Sam's neck, and the entire room shifted. "This is none of your concern."

"Isn't it?" My tone changed from deceptively light to viperous. Simmering anger coiled my muscles and galvanized every step. Most of it was me. I loved Sam and would kill anyone who tried to harm her. But there was demon in my motions. The monster inside bombarded me with another scene—my fist repeatedly pummeling the guy as he begged for mercy. The tantalizing lure of blood and fear and rage was almost too compelling to resist, but somehow I managed to push down the itch. *Sam*. Had to focus on Sam. I nodded to her. "You okay?"

"Well, you know…" Sam was tougher than any ten women put together, still there was the slightest shake to her voice. Gray smoke bled into the air around her and almost sent me over the edge. "I'm not really into this guy, but he won't take no for an answer."

The demon's hunger caused pin pricks of pain to bloom across my body. Killing this asshole would be easy. I could get in and remove him from the situation without mussing Sam's hair. But how the fuck was I going to explain a dead body in the storage room? My new boss wouldn't like it.

I caught Sam's gaze and gave a slight nod upward. Whoever had stocked the vodka shelf had been lazy. The bottles were all perilously close to the edge directly above where the guy was standing. She tilted her head, but I had no idea if she saw it or not.

"You're still here," he said. There was something about his voice that bothered me. The underlying tone, while distinctly human, was just slightly…off.

"So are you," Sam snapped. She brought her leg up and slammed it back into the wooden shelving. Glass clattered overhead and several of the bottles teetered and fell. They hit their mark and the guy went down hard, glass shattering all around him, clear liquid splashing everywhere.

"Hope you were thirsty," Sam said. "I suppose I should thank—"

The guy lifted his head and made a grab for her ankle. Sam yelped in surprise and kicked him hard. His eyes rolled back and he went still at her feet. Unfortunately her movement jostled the shelf again. The last remaining bottle of vodka wobbled, then plummeted.

I pitched forward, fingers closing around the bottle seconds before it crashed into her head. "…you," she finished softly.

My face was inches from hers, and her breath, sweetened by the rum punch she'd been sneaking all night, puffed across my face. I took her arm and dragged her around the corner to the next row of shelves. Common sense said to pull away, to move to the other end of the room where I could maintain a safe amount of space between us.

I didn't.

Azi was pleased. A series of disturbing and enticing pictures swam through my head. Lush caramel hair and big brown eyes. Creamy skin, warm beneath my fingers. A sound, delicate yet more powerful than any force of nature. My name spoken by a familiar feminine voice. Goose bumps rose along my skin and my heart raced. It was all fake. An illusion created by the demon in order to incite a reaction. But the scenes were like 3D movies, a kick to the nuts with five-inch spurs. *Dig in and twist.* I felt them, smelled them, and too often found myself unable to resist reacting to them.

"What the hell were you thinking?" I pushed the pictures aside and focused on the real Sam, the one in front of me. "Coming down to the basement with some random guy? After all the shit that's gone down recently? Are you—" I jabbed my finger at her attackers, but both the guy and the girl were gone. "What the fuck?"

Sam peered around the corner, then back to me, brows knitted together. She turned in a slow circle, scanning the rest of the room, confused. "Must have run out the basement door."

"Must have run—" I grabbed her arm and pinned her against the wall. "This is the fifth time in a month that we've had a problem, Sammy."

"I work in a club." She was defensive, but I heard the underlying concern. "There are going to be minor problems."

I leaned in close, much closer than I should have dared. "Getting hit on is a minor problem. Having some dickhead puke on you is a minor problem. Being repeatedly attacked is *not* a minor problem."

She grabbed a handful of my T-shirt and graced me with a grin that set my insides on fire. "Well then, I guess you'll have to pay closer attention to me, huh?"

It didn't seem fair that with one look this girl could completely unravel me, make me forget the world and lose myself in the simple sound of her voice. The demon wanted me to push forward, but I resisted. Being this close to Sam had disaster smeared all over it.

Unfortunately, thanks to the demon, every sense, each nerve ending, was magnified. I was hyperaware of every breath. The subtle tug at the neckline of her shirt as she crossed her arms. The slight shift of her weight as she leaned back against the wall.

Another round of images from Azi blotted out reality for a moment. It showed Sam on the floor, back arched and head thrown back as she writhed beneath me. Begging.

I was instantly hard.

The vision faded, and she sighed. "We should probably get back to work. Or…" Her hands came to my chest. The warmth seeping through the thin, cheap black T-shirt was like an inferno burning straight to my soul. My heart slammed against my ribs as she pushed off the wall and rose onto her toes.

Still. Had to stay perfectly still. One wrong move and…

With her lips lingering at my ear, her hot breath melting what little resolve I had, she whispered, "You could put your hands all over me."

Fuck…

"You need to stop." I forced her away. "We can't do this."

We'd been playing a dangerous game the last few weeks. Toeing the line. A stolen look here. A brush of skin there. Things had to change or I was going to do something that would land us both in trouble.

Sam folded her arms. Even in the shitty basement light, her swirling colors were easily visible. The orange of lust and red of anger were burning beacons against the darkness, tantalizing in a way that almost made me forget the rules and take what I wanted. Her. "Then why are you still standing there?"

Because there was no such thing as self-control when it came to her.

And that had to change.

"You want me," she said when I didn't answer. The orange smoke thickened, becoming more alluring.

"Not the point," I responded, but my body ignored the words. I licked my lips and, giving into the pull, stepped closer. Martin, the club owner, had instated a new dress code for the bartenders. He insisted they wear short black skirts instead of the previously approved jeans. Sam hated showing too much skin. She'd gotten around it by wearing tall boots, leaving only a small section of creamy thigh exposed. If even possible, it was sexier, giving just a seductive tease of the treasure that lay beneath.

Being so close, I found it impossible not to touch. My hands drifted down, playing with the edge of the silky material for a moment before tugging it up. First a fraction of an inch. Then a little bit more. The skin was soft. Inviting. I imagined what it would be like to run my tongue across and upward, until I came to her center. Then I—

Sam tilted her head back and let out a small sigh, and Azi went wild. It took in the swirl of lust and greedily inhaled. I wasn't unaffected. The demon needed the emotion to survive. It was sustenance. To me it was like a drug, and even though I despised myself, the sickest parts of me loved it.

Craved it.

Sam's hands covered mine, urging them—and the skirt— higher. Along with the demon I breathed in deeply, letting the orange mist envelope me. It was a heady sensation, one I knew to be dangerous. Losing myself in her, in her emotions, was one of my triggers, one turn of the key that blocked my control over the demon.

I groaned. There was nothing more I wanted than to give in and do all the dirty, twisted things clanking around my brain since the last time—the only time—we'd been together, but it couldn't happen. Not now. When I'd come back to town a few months ago, it had stirred up a whirlwind of shit. In order to save ourselves—and the world—Sam and I had called on powerful help, which hadn't come for free. We were still paying the price.

I yanked my hands away. "You're making this ten times harder on both of us," I snapped. Azi, realizing that I wasn't going to give in to temptation, grew angry as well, fueling my own fury and frustration. "How fucking hard do you think it is for me to stay in this damn town knowing that you're off-limits? To have you right in front of me and not be able to—"

She opened her mouth, but I covered her lips with my hand. The last thing I needed right then was the sound of her voice. It would push me over the edge.

"You're everywhere. In my house, at my work—"

She pried my hand away and fixed those beautiful brown eyes on me. "Your work? Technically I was here—"

I covered her mouth again. "Everywhere except where I want you. In my bed. In my fucking life."

She pulled my hand away again, and this time I let her. My resolve was crumbling. "I'm in your life, Jax. No deal is ever going to change that. We need to readjust. Find a new normal. Something that will work for this…situation. Maybe it's time for me to move out of the house. I've saved a little bit of money. Chase has been gone for—"

"No." Sam moved into my Uncle Rick's house in case more trouble came beating down her door. It was a multipurpose choice. She'd been kicked out of her old place and needed somewhere to stay, and having her close so I could keep an eye out made me feel better. We'd only intended it to be temporary. Living under the same roof was like spreading a feast in front of a starving man. But the thought of not having her there was more agonizing.

I was a masochist. Clearly.

"No," I spat again. "That's not what—"

"Well then, where's the line?" she asked, pushing forward until she was pressed against me. I held my breath. "*You gave me up*. That's what you told me, right?"

Sam had sacrificed her life to break a demonic link between her and Chase, allowing me to beat the shit out of him. But it hadn't been enough. My brother—who'd been hiding his own demon—had been in synch with it from the time he was a kid, and they didn't have a fair fight in mind. I'd needed more of an edge. That's where the deal came in. I'd leveled the playing field but had to sacrifice the only thing I loved. Sam. Now, as further payment, we were both bound by our word to serve as "agents of balance"—though the broker of the deal hadn't bothered to tell us yet what the fuck that meant.

"Right," I replied, letting out my breath. I held it that way, not daring to breathe in.

Her voice dropped. She shifted, rubbing against me, and I clenched my jaw tight. "But we're supposed to be partners, correct?"

"Correct," I confirmed tightly.

"And we live together. So, us spending time together obviously *isn't* against the rules." She wrapped an arm around my neck and pulled my head down so that our foreheads touched. "That's all we're doing here. Spending time…"

Something inside me cracked. I brought my lips to her earlobe, skimming the smooth skin. "Do you get off on pushing me?" I growled. My own colors swirled, a maelstrom of deep red and orange that mingled with hers. "Testing the limits of my restraint?"

My arms encircled her, hands sliding down to her ass. I gripped hard, pulling her into me, and a shock of sensation hit like lightning. Pain roared to life in my muscles. When I was close to Sam, I was happy. Azi didn't do happy. It caused the demon pain, which also caused me pain. It wasn't as bad as it used to be, but it was still there. I didn't care, though. Neither did the demon. We both wanted nothing more than to be close to her.

She shimmied and a soft laugh escaped her lips. "What would you do if I said ye—"

I crushed my lips to hers. The demon rumbled, triumphant. I'd never been one to welsh on a deal, but I just didn't give a shit. It would have been easy to blame my lack of restraint on Azi. Since the night Sam and I had sex, it had been pushing for more, making me desperate to a point that I found myself watching her move across a room, counting the ways I could take her, all the things I could do.

Sam moaned into my mouth. The sound was like ten thousand jolts of electricity hitting at once, and it pushed me over the edge. I thrust myself against her, sending waves of current pulsating through my body. I pulled away for a second, mouth lingering at her ear again. With a dark laugh, I whispered, "I'd say it was a good way to get yourself fu—"

A rushing sensation filled my head. The link Sam had unwittingly created between us flared to life, bringing about a *moment*—what we'd started calling the visions that sometimes came from our contact. She stood at the window of her old room in her Aunt Kelly's house. She stared at the house next door, the window across from hers dark and silent. Tears slid down her cheeks. The sadness she felt was overwhelming, strong enough to make me cringe.

Reality came crashing back, and I made a move to pull away. I didn't get the chance.

The stairs creaked, followed by the steady echo of footsteps. Sam jerked away and gasped. "Oh my God."

"Not quite," said an ominously familiar voice.

Chapter Two

Sam

I stumbled away from Jax, who'd thrown a protective arm in front of me.

"But that's probably a good thing." Chase, Jax's mirror image, stood by the door with his arms folded. He wiggled a finger between us and winked — a comfortable, familiar gesture that almost made me forget he was the enemy. "I heard this was a no-no."

I swallowed the newly formed lump in my throat. A part of me wanted to reach out and pinch him to see if he was real. Because he couldn't be, right? Lies, attempted murder, and all-around chaos… He'd have to be a special kind of moron to show his face here after what he'd done.

Or, be packing a serious advantage.

Jax wasn't the only Flynn sporting a dark side. His twin brother Chase's demon, Zenak, was Azi's sworn enemy. A pair of demon royals, their pissing contest went a little too far once, and they'd been exiled to spend eternity trapped in a continuous string of human bodies.

The Flynn boys had fought a battle of apocalyptic proportions, but Chase, the sneaky bastard, linked himself to me—a parasitic and creeptastic bond that made him untouchable. I'd had to essentially commit suicide in order for Jax to defeat him.

Backing away, I tried not to flinch. I'd known the two boys since I was six. Chase was every inch the predator Jax was. He could smell weakness from a mile away. "Why ever you're here, just forget it…"

"Let me guess." Chase unfolded his arms and waggled his finger at the floor. "He was helping you find your contact lens, right?"

From the look on Jax's face, he was about to reach critical mass. If it'd been anyone else, he might have ripped into flesh and asked questions later, but he had a bit more restraint when it came to his brother. Not because of some sappy fraternal bond, but because Chase's death—or his own—would herald a demonic apocalypse. The standoff—hell, the whole demonic war—defined a no-win situation. Not that either brother would back down.

Jax made a noise low in his throat and dragged me behind him. "Chase—"

He threw his hands in the air and shook his head. "Peace, brother. I'm not here to make trouble."

"Kind of hard to believe," I mumbled.

"So is the fact that you're here." Chase folded his arms, cocky grin still in place. It was hard to reconcile that this was the enemy standing in front of me and not one of my closest friends. When Jax left home, Chase had been my rock, the shoulder I cried on and the support that made it possible for me to move forward with my life. But mind control and attempted murder tended to ruin a friendship. "Pretty sure the last time I saw you, you were dead."

I opened my mouth—to say what, I had no clue—but never got a chance to speak. Jax lunged forward and wrapped his fingers around Chase's neck. With a graceful pivot, he had their positions reversed, his brother flush against the wall with his feet dangling about a foot off the ground. "What do you want?"

Chase, always amused by Jax's ferocity, let out a strangled chuckle. "Put me…down…and…tell you."

I was pretty sure Jax squeezed just a bit harder before finally setting his brother on his feet.

Chase smoothed out his black button-down shirt and rolled his shoulders. With a wink to me he said, "Don't act all murder and mayhem. If you were going to kill me, you would have done it months ago."

Jax glowered. "Careful. I might have reconsidered."

Chase wasn't convinced—and rightly so. The demon Azirak had lived a thousand lives since its banishment from hell. While it wanted to see its clan restored to their former glory, the demon knew what that would do to the world. Maybe it'd gone soft. Or, maybe it liked what it had going in its current incarnation. It seemed that, like Jax, Azirak had developed certain…feelings for me. Enough that it didn't wish to see me trampled under the weight of its demonic horde.

Chase turned away from Jax, fixing his gaze on me. A flash of regret, there and gone in an instant, and he was smiling again. "Well, however you managed it, I have to say, Samantha, it's good to see you alive."

I waved my hand. "Wish I could say the same, but…"

"Yeah, yeah," he retorted. "And now that the formalities are out of the way, we might as well get down to it." He nodded over his shoulder at Jax. "I doubt his patience has improved since embracing the demon."

"Last time, Chase. What the fuck do you want?"

The music from the main floor drifted down, the beat

changing slightly as one song faded seamlessly into the next. Chase sighed. "We're never going to be good again, Samantha. I know that. And I get it. But I'm here to try and give you back at least a little bit of what I took."

"What you took?" I asked, skeptical. I wasn't sure what he was talking about. He'd betrayed me. His brother, too. He'd caused a ton of pain and essentially tried to end the world. But he hadn't stolen anything as far as I knew.

Jax was tense, but quiet. Chase took it as a sign to continue. "I might be able to offer a solution to your…problem."

"Problem?" Jax was instantly alert. He pushed me aside. "Which one would that be? The demons or you?"

"I won't apologize for what I did. The demon's nature is my nature and has been since the moment I embraced it. That nature takes precedence over the fact that you were once my brother."

"You're not helping your argument," Jax snarled, taking a step closer. His movements were fluid and menacing. Controlled, with deadly intent.

"Get to the point, Chase," I interjected, trying to keep things on track.

"My point is that my problem is with him." He hitched his thumb at Jax then turned to me. "Not you."

"So what exactly are you saying?" I hated to admit it, but all this talk was making me nervous. What if this was a ploy to buy time, and any second, twenty demons would ambush us. It wouldn't be the first time he'd done something like that.

"I'm saying I'm sorry you were dragged into this," said Chase. "That your life was affected. I'm sorry I tried to use you to get to him. Zenak may have no use for you, but believe it or not, I care. It bothers me to know that you're in pain."

"Pain?" I repeated, even more suspicious.

"Word travels. I know what he sacrificed to gain Heckle's aid. I know what *he*"—he nodded at Jax—"had to give up."

"I find it hard to believe you're bummed because Jax and I can't be together." Even though we were living with it day in and out, hearing someone else speak it out loud was a fresh set of knives twisting in my heart.

He shrugged. "I saw how you suffered when he left the first time. I watched you miss him all those years. I'm not heartless, Samantha. He's an ass, but for some reason you still want him."

Jax snorted. "So you came back to town—a risky move, by the way—to what? Play supernatural cupid?"

Chase eyed him, clenching his jaw. He took a visible breath, and I realized this must be just as hard for him as it was for Jax, standing here without tearing into his brother. "I came to give you something. A name."

"A name?"

"There's a demon in town. A real badass. Serious trouble."

Jax took another step closer. "There are a lot of demons in town. Why should I care?"

"This one is different. *Malphi* is particularly nasty. Who knows? Maybe Heckle will reward you for taking it out. Lift the…" He gestured to us. "The no-touching rule he put in place when you made your little deal."

Jax was quiet, but I couldn't keep my mouth closed. Selfless had never been Chase's style. "What are *you* getting out of this?"

He didn't even try hiding it. "Naturally, the death of this demon is beneficial to me as well."

"And there it is," Jax snapped.

"This demon, Malphi, is trouble for both of us, Jax. It needs to be taken out."

Jax jabbed a finger at the stairs. "Then why don't you take care of it?"

"I told you. If you take it down—"

"Yeah. Bargaining chip. I heard you the first time. I just

don't buy it."

"He can't take this thing down on his own," I said. Despite the secrets he'd kept from me, I knew Chase. His human side, at least. He was manipulative and greedy but, above all else, worried about one thing—himself. "*That's* why he's here. This isn't an olive branch—it's self-preservation."

"It's a little bit of that, too." Chase gave a sly grin.

"Sucks for you," Jax said. A truly wicked smile spread across his face as he leaned in close to his brother. "Good luck with your demon. The answer is no."

"But—"

"It's not going to happen, Chase," I said. There was no way this was anything more than a ploy to get us to do his dirty work. If Malphi even existed, then Chase had done something to piss it off, and now he was running scared and looking for someone to clean up his mess.

"I was afraid you'd say that." He sighed and shot forward. One moment he stood in front of Jax, the next he was beside me, fingers wrapped like a vise around my wrist. It all took place in a matter of moments. His movement. Jax tearing him away and tossing his body across the room. The new, heavy weight around my wrist...

"What the hell?" It was a shiny black metal band decorated with strange symbols. They were slightly raised, and as I watched they seemed to flash several times before going dormant.

Chase picked himself off the floor and smoothed the front of his shirt. "Oh, that? It's called a demon cuff, and if it's not removed, it will kill you." He turned to Jax. "So, care to reconsider?"

Chapter Three

Jax

R ed bled through my vision, and I lunged for my brother. "What the fuck did you do?"

"Easy, man. Kill me and not only does your clan rise and wreak havoc, but she'll die a particularly nasty death."

I tore my gaze from him. "Sammy?"

"I dunno..." Her voice was hesitant. She flexed her hand, wiggling each of her fingers. Whispers of gray, of fear, filled the small space between the two shelves. They curled upward and thickened, and with the link between us, it was almost all I could focus on. "I feel...weird."

Chase noticed, too. He took a deep breath and gave a contented sigh. "Fear isn't as good as lust, but still tasty, right?"

I pushed him away and moved to stand beside Sam. The cuff didn't look like much, but one touch and I felt it hum with power. "Take it off. Now."

"No way." Chase shook his head. He took a step back. "I wasn't lying about Malphi. It's a danger to both of us.

Samantha, too."

She narrowed her eyes. "And of course Jax taking this demon out makes your life easier, right?"

"Killing it does him just as much good as it does me." He shrugged and moved carefully toward the door with slow, measured movements, never taking his eyes off mine. "You've got a few choices here, Jax. Can't say I envy you. You can kill me now and unleash hell on earth. Samantha will die and Azirak will take over completely. You can do nothing. Malphi lives, Samantha dies. We'll all probably die. Or, you can kill Malphi. I will remove the cuff, and everyone gets what they want."

"Those aren't choices," Sam snapped. "This whole thing is one big trap."

Chase frowned. I'd seen the look a million times growing up, but I'd never noticed the lack of sincerity until right then. "This is no trap, Samantha. Really, if you think about it, I did you a favor."

"A favor?" she yelled, and I grabbed her arm as a preventive measure. The explosion of red, along with the weight of her fury hitting me through the link, told me she was seconds away from lunging for him. "You sonofa—"

"Malphi would have taken you by surprise had I not brought the danger to your attention. So, yeah. I did you a solid." He turned to me. "Both of you. Time to repay the favor."

There wasn't any part of me that didn't want him dead in that moment. My human and demon side were in total agreement. To hell with the consequences. Fuck the fact that it would destroy the world as we knew it. He kept crossing me. Kept getting in my way and trying to ruin what little peace I'd gained.

But it was the unadulterated fear coming from Sam, in the air and in the link, that stopped me from acting on my growing bloodlust. Her eyes, so full of dread, were glued to

Chase, like she was trying to decide if this was all just some bad dream.

Chase was smart. He'd done it again. Used Sam to steer me in the direction he wanted me to go. I was cornered and he knew it. "If you can't kill the demon, what makes you think that I can?"

"You're resourceful, Jax. Plus…" He inclined his head toward Sam. There was hunger in his eyes. "You have powerful motivation. Maybe your buddy Heckle will help. You don't know it yet, but he owes you." With a shrug, he added, "Of course, I'll need proof the demon is dead." He tipped his head and thought about it for a moment. "How about this? Malphi wears a red stone around its neck. Get me that stone and I'll know the deed is done. I'll remove the cuff."

"Oh, now there's a stone, too?" Sam cried. "Because that sounds like a great idea. What's it do, Chase? Because I'll wager nine of my ten fingers that it's not just a simple rock."

I squeezed her hand. "What's to stop me from stealing the stone and leaving the demon?"

Chase laughed. "Impossible. That rock isn't coming off until Malphi is dead. It's…shall we say, the demon's security blanket." The top right hand corner of his lip curled upward as he started up the stairs. "And Jax?"

I glared at him, with Azi flashing a barrage of images involving my fist repeatedly pummeling his face.

"This is a limited time offer. The cuff is only removable within the first seventy-two hours."

"Three days?" Sam squawked. "How are we supposed to find this thing in three days?"

Chase winked then opened the door. Right before he slipped through, he said, "I wouldn't worry, Samantha. Malphi will probably find *you*."

Every time Chase had mentioned Malphi's name, Azirak reacted strangely, restless and bristling. I got the feeling it knew of the demon, and judging by its reaction we had our work cut out for us. It had been oddly quiet since Chase left. That bothered me but not as much as watching Sam from across the dance floor. She was talking to the other bartender as she slipped into her jacket. Waves of gray swirled around her head and shoulders, a storm of fear that almost swallowed her small frame. We'd told the boss that a family member had been in an accident. The sooner we went to work fixing this, the better I'd feel.

I didn't believe in that love-at-first-sight shit, but I'd known Sam was special the instant we met. Both carrying the weight of the world on our shoulders, even at that young age, we were two parts of the same whole. We'd grown up inseparable. More than friends. Sam was my lifeline, tethering me to reality. The only bright light in an existence cloaked in darkness. As a teenager, I finally found the balls to admit what she meant to me, and it'd changed everything.

My feelings for her drove the demon inside me insane. It pushed my control over the edge and left me teetering on the verge of madness. So to shield her, and everyone else I loved, I'd left her behind. Packed a bag and snuck away in the dead of night without saying good-bye. Then a few months ago, fate shoved us together again. I thought maybe I'd finally get a shot with her. I'd been wrong. The universe seemed to be working against us, but together or not, this world would be cold and dark without someone like Sam in it. I wasn't about to let that happen.

"Ready?" she called over the music as she crossed the floor. "Heckle is probably our best bet at the moment. He might know exactly what this is. Maybe even be able to take it off." She gave her wrist a slight shake. If possible, the plume of gray around her head grew even larger, and it took all my willpower not to give in to the demon. It was frantic, desperate to feed and fighting for control. Right now Sam was a succulent buffet with a neon sign that read *Free Food*.

"Yeah." We wove through the crowd and slipped out the door, past a large crowd waiting to get in. I'd left the car in the lot behind the building.

Heckle *was* the way to go, but right now I had to be as far from Sam as possible. We needed to deal with the cuff, but in order to do that, I needed to feed. *Now*. The link hadn't settled, and the extra push I was getting from her was driving me insane. Handing her the car keys, I took a long step back. "I'll meet you back at the house."

She looked down at my hand, then up again without reaching for the keys. "Meet me back at the house? You're staying here?"

"No," I said, taking another step away. I didn't trust myself—or Azi. In addition to Chase's impromptu visit and the fear he'd stirred up, I was still charged from being so close to her in the basement. If I allowed myself to be alone with her, I wouldn't be able to control my actions—or the demon's. I was a walking grenade and the pin had been pulled. "I'm going back to the house. Just not with you."

Her expression chilled the air. She was angry, but more than that, hurt. Because of me. My words. My actions. No matter what my intentions were, I was beginning to realize that it would always be this way. Something I said, something I did—what I was—would always end up hurting her.

"You're going to what, walk? Flap your arms and fly home? Am I missing something here?" She thrust her wrist at me. "We kind of have an issue."

"I know. And yeah, I'm going to walk," I snapped, feeling like an asshole. I threw the keys at her and she caught them, mouth falling open. "Is that a problem?"

Her surprise only lasted a second. The shock turned to

anger, and she fired the keys back, twice as hard. The days of me pushing her away by being a dick were gone. She knew the game and refused to play. But her reaction was normally less volatile. "What the hell?"

The keys fell to the ground with a clatter that echoed through the alley, and all I wanted to do was scream. At her. At Heckle. At life. She didn't deserve that because this wasn't her fault. It was mine. And even though I knew that, it was impossible to keep my anger in check. It was happening more and more since I'd embraced the demon, little random flickers of rage that became jets of all-consuming flame. Moments where it all got away from me.

But this was different. This was all me. "I don't want to be cooped up in a confined space with you right now, *okay*?" I took a deep breath, then blew out slowly, trying to get myself under control. "If I don't feed Azi, I'm going to lose my shit."

She held my gaze for a minute, eyes full of uncharacteristic fury, then bent to retrieve the keys with a jerk. She wanted to hit me. Scream and rage until the anger faded and there was no energy left to expend. The potency of it slammed through me, nearly stealing the breath from my lungs. Without thinking, I grabbed her hand.

The alley next to the Viking fell away. Sam was still in front of me, but she was with someone else. A tall guy with a spider tattoo on his forearm. He leaned in to kiss her and I felt my body coil, ready to pounce. But before I could act, the scene shimmered and faded, and it was Sam and I again outside the Viking.

The *moments* that resulted from our link were mostly innocuous scenes from the past, but once in a while, the visions were intense, coupled with a full gamut of debilitating emotion. Eventually one of us was going to see something that did some real damage.

We still didn't understand it all. Some demons could create

a link to their victims, constructing a parasitic relationship that benefited them at a horrible expense to the human. But this was different.

First, Sam wasn't a demon. She was…something else, but we had no clue what. Also, unlike with a demonic link, there didn't appear to be any adverse effects—at first. A few weeks ago, things began to change. We'd become more in tune with each other's moods. It was subtle at first. So brief that we both thought we were imagining things. The frequency seemed to be increasing, though it was still random.

In that moment—at the look in her eyes—if she had begged me to get in the car, I would have without hesitation. Thankfully she was stronger than me. Without a word, she slid into Rick's old clunker, slammed the door, and started the engine. The inside of the cab flooded with red as she peeled from of the lot, so thick I could barely make out her silhouette. I hated that she felt that way, but it was a relief. Anger, in my book, was always better than hurt. It was easier to deal with. To conquer. Anger fueled you. It could poison you if allowed to run rampant, or drive you if it remained focused.

I just wasn't sure whose emotions I was fighting anymore—mine or hers.

I walked the streets of Harlow for hours before catching a whiff of fear, four miles from the club. When I went to investigate, I found a guy trying to steal some lady's purse as she unpacked suitcases from the trunk of her car.

While I couldn't go as far with a human as I could a demon—killing the demonic bastards left me with one hell of a high and virtually no guilt—I could rough them up enough to calm Azi for a time and gain a small amount of peace.

After giving the scumbag a proper beat down, I went in

search of answers. Heckle owned a bar in downtown Harlow, The Inferno. Unfortunately, the man behind the bar wasn't him. All he would tell me was that Heckle was away and he had no idea when he would return. After a few rounds of Q and A—the kind that involved pain and bloodshed—I started for Rick's.

An hour after getting home and trying repeatedly to reach Heckle's cell, I gave up. Wherever he was, he wasn't interested in chatting. I knew I should try to catch a few hours of sleep then tackle this thing with a clearer head in the morning. But it was impossible. Each time I closed my eyes, Azi flooded my mind with images. They ranged from raw, animalistic sex to wicked teasing, all with the same effect. The thing was relentless and I was on fire. It wasn't long before I found myself standing outside Sam's door, hands braced against the frame and fingers digging into the molding. It took all my willpower not to bust through and—

"Since we're both awake, you might as well just come in," she said softly. She was inside the room, behind the closed door, but since embracing the demon, I couldn't turn off the heightened senses it afforded me. Before, I'd had to surrender a certain amount of control to the monster to gain access to its more than human abilities. But since turning myself over to it, I had full access without the surrender. It'd been disorienting at first—hearing the heartbeat of everyone in a room, or the sound of their breath as it moved in and out of their lungs—but I'd gotten it under control for the most part.

Except when it came to Sam. I was hyperaware of her all the time. The way she moved, and the subtle hitches in her voice as her mood changed. Being so in tune with the one person I couldn't get close to was a fresh kind of torture every day.

I sucked in a breath and pushed open the door. Sam was in bed with the covers pooled around her waist. The small lamp on the nightstand beside the bed illuminated her features, accentuating each curve in sharp, painful detail.

"I owe you an—"

"Don't." She held up her hand. "I get it, and I *hate* it. But...I get it."

Of course she did. Always so damn understanding. Everything from my mood swings to the blood that always seemed to stain my hands—Sam was able to look past all of it, and a part of me hated her for it. I was a bastard. A monster unworthy of redemption. If I could get her to see that, to believe it, then it would be true.

But she didn't. She wouldn't. When she looked at me, there was nothing but love and optimism, and it was exhausting, trying to live up to her expectations and knowing it was impossible.

She shifted and the covers fell to the side, revealing a glimpse of her leg. Azi stirred, flashing images of creamy skin and supple curves, ripe beneath my fingers. I swallowed.

"Inviting me in here was a bad idea." My pulse jumped and the air heated. Every breath she took echoed inside my head, a siren's song with the ability to control my every move.

She shoved the covers away, swinging her long legs over the edge. Blue tank top and barely-there panties. Fuck.

"We're more than this, Jax." She crossed the room to where I stood, moving deliberately slow and swinging her hips. With her index finger, she traced a path from my chin to my ear, along my jawline. The sensation was euphoric. "We're more than stolen moments and forbidden touches." She grabbed my hand and placed it over her heart. "You're my other half."

Pulse thundering in my ears, I tried to focus on her words and not the way her lips looked as they moved. Not the memory of what they tasted like, or how they felt—sinfully soft and electric—pressed against mine. Not the slight curve of her breast, so close to where my hand lay. "I want you."

"Do you?" Her hand, still atop mine, moved south a few inches until my fingers rested against the underside of her breast. She rose onto her toes and whispered at my ear, her voice low and breathless, "I couldn't tell…"

This time the demon didn't need to taunt me. The thoughts came all on their own, a series of mouthwatering scenarios that all involved Sam naked, in various positions, screaming my name. It was more than I could take. I grabbed her shoulders and reversed our position, spinning her toward the wall and pinning her there with the length of my body. I was straddling the line, and all it would take to push me over was the smallest nudge. One she seemed intent on providing.

"I could take you." Hard, I ground myself against her, the friction sending an even mixture of pleasure and pain coursing through me.

There was a wicked grin on her lips, and a strong sense of satisfaction surged through the link. She *wanted* to push me. To send me over the edge.

With a soft, pleading moan, she let her head fall back against the wall. The sound turned everything dark. I lost focus. Lost where I was and what I was doing. A small nagging voice in the back of my head that told me this wasn't right, that Sam wouldn't push me like this, but it was eclipsed by blind lust. The desire was so potent I could taste it, sharp and acidic, so unshakable I found myself helpless. A slave to it.

The demon was right there with me.

"*We* could do anything and *everything* that we wanted, and you would like it." All that existed in that moment was Sam and the unbearable need. Something gnawed at my subconscious. A thought too dim to recognize. A warning… It wasn't important. The urge to satisfy the darkest fantasies we both had for this woman overshadowed everything. To take her. Possess her. "You would *beg* for it."

"Careful," she whispered fervently. "You're coming undone—"

I grabbed a handful of her hair and braced my fist against the wall, securing her there. "Isn't that what you wanted?" I growled. Leaning in, I skimmed the line of her jaw, nipping lightly at the skin as I made my way down, around to her collarbone.

She arched against me, a soft rumble in her throat. Her hands tangled in my hair.

Azi sent an image. Me taking Sam. Hard. Fast. Possessive and feral... No. Not me. Azirak. I watched as the picture played out, mesmerized by the ferocity of it. Prurient grunting and a feminine groan that made me hard as rock and ready to explode. I was enthralled. Captivated by the savagery of the scene.

Vision-Sam cried out. Except it wasn't her voice I heard. It was something deeper, a sound far too harsh to have come from human lips. The vision changed. It was still me, but Sam was gone. Beneath me was something shadowed. A form distinctly female, but not human. Not one I knew, yet one I wanted to devour.

A flash of dark hair and pale skin. Large, full breasts bounced as I rammed myself violently forward, sinking into warmth. I growled, a feral, inhuman sound that mingled with the moans of excitement coming from the thing beneath me. The sensation that came over me, a savage desire unlike anything else I'd ever experienced, needed to be sated.

The vision ended, but the feeling it left behind was all consuming. It left me raw, an exposed nerve throbbing for release. Words spilled from my lips, too soft for human ears, syllables and sounds I didn't understand but physically hurt to hear. I buried my face in Sam's neck, running my tongue from her cheek to collarbone. One taste wasn't enough. I wanted more. *Needed it.*

I raked my fingers down her body, to her backside, and hefted her off the ground. In response she wrapped both legs tight around my waist. I crossed the room and threw her onto the bed. The frame groaned and something metallic snapped. I didn't care. The visions started again and even though every inch of my mind was telling me to stop, my body refused to listen.

"Jax," Sam panted. A whisper of gray swirled, mingling with the thick orange. "Maybe we—"

I covered her mouth with mine to silence her. She tasted like lust. Lust and fear... I breathed it in, desperate for more, while in the back of my mind I was horrified. The fear. I craved it almost as much as I craved her touch. A rush of possibilities clamored through my head. Ways I could increase the potency. Things I could do to scare her...

What the fuck was I doing?

I jumped up and backed myself into the opposite corner of the room, breath coming in shallow pulls. My stomach tightened.

Sam sat up and started toward me. "What are you—"

"Stop," I roared. She froze, and I squeezed my eyes closed for a second. Everything was spinning. The images hadn't stopped. In one after another, I watched myself take what I wanted from her, satisfying the demon's sickest whims. In my mind she screamed and cried and begged me to stop. Then in an instant, she was cooing and pleading for more. Back and forth. Pleasure and pain. "The pictures... They're dark and vicious. Possessive. I wanted to hurt you, Sammy. To taste your fear."

"Fear? Jax, I could never be af—"

I slammed my fists backward into the wall behind me. The plaster crumbled beneath the blow, showering the carpet with dust and debris. "Yes!" The word ripped from my throat, bouncing like a stray bullet off the walls of her small room. I took a step forward, goaded by the look of surprise on her face. My lips spread with a grin. "I could make you afraid. I could do things that would terrify you."

Her skin paled. This time, instead of coming closer, she had the sense to back away. Two steps to the right, then around the bottom of the bed until she was on the other side. "This isn't you talking, Jax. It's Azi."

"Maybe it is," I admitted, even though I couldn't be sure anymore. The line between the demon and I grew hazier each day. I'd never admit it, but I worried one day it would disappear all together, leaving us a single creature. "But some small part is me. *I* liked what I saw, Sammy. I *needed* it."

"I don't believe that," she said, resolute.

"Listen to me!" I shouted. This was serious. I wanted Sam. In every way, I wanted her. But she was more to me than the desire she sparked. She was home. My best friend. To have so little control over my impulses meant Azi *was* stronger than I'd anticipated. Even now there was very little keeping me from closing the distance between her and...

Deep breath. "I'm having a hard time controlling myself around you. I saw..."

What had I seen? The fire I'd felt for the thing in the vision still burned in my veins, tangled with my desire for Sam. It left me raw and exposed.

"I don't care what you saw," she said softly. One foot in front of the other, she cautiously made her way around the bed to where I stood and took my hands. They looked huge in hers—calloused, rough things brushing against perfect creamy satin. "You never give yourself enough credit, Jax. You are the strongest man I know."

Strong? She was fucking insane. My heart thundered, the erratic rhythm making it impossible to draw anything more than quick, shallow breaths that did little to satisfy my need for air. The walls seemed to be closing in. The room to be growing smaller. Need. There was something I needed.

Something that would make this suffocating feeling go away.

Sam shook her head. "Jax…"

I grabbed her arms and pinned them behind her. Control. The desire to dominate. She needed to know that she was *mine*. "You belong to me," I whispered fiercely, working my way down her neck. I wasn't gentle. Taking small sections of skin between my teeth, I nipped and twisted. Not hard enough to be painful, but with enough force to make her gasp. To drive my point home. "You belong to me. *Mine*," I said, pulling away.

Any reservations she might have had after my sickening confession seemed to melt into nothingness. She pushed forward. I felt her eagerness. To taste me again. To feel me pressed against her. *Inside* her. But I held her back. At arm's length, my hands still knotted in her hair, I kept her secure.

"You understand me, right?" My fingers twitched, tightening, and a flash of that same dark female figure almost brought me to my knees.

Sam nodded, slowly, then jerked forward. I let go of her hair, surprised, as she grabbed either side of my neck, her nails digging into the skin. Stopping a fraction of an inch from my lips, she said, her voice low and hypnotic, "*Understand* that it works both ways."

Fuck…

She bit at my bottom lip, then wriggled her hands up beneath my shirt, dragging her nails hard across the skin. The pain drove Azi wild. It just about got me off, too. My hands fell to my zipper.

My entire body ached to be inside her, and the image of that female, still too fresh in my mind, needed to be scrubbed away. This would be the thing to do it—replacing that scene with one of my making. One of my choosing. I leaned in again, determined to do this despite Heckle's warnings, but…

Something crashed outside the room.

Chapter Four

Jax was at the door in an instant. "Stay here," he barked over his shoulder. I opened my mouth to argue, but he slipped from the room, dismissing me.

Oh, hell no.

I yanked open the door and followed.

A few steps ahead of me, he rounded the corner and rushed into the hallway between the living room and kitchen, where it sounded like the noise had come from. When I caught up to him he was in the doorway. The glass above the door on the other side of the kitchen was shattered—a million tiny pieces lay on the floor. "What happened?"

Jax whirled around, eyes narrow. "I told you to—"

Something flew at us from the right. We were knocked apart like bowling pins, but somehow I managed to stay upright. Not Jax, though. He went down hard with a grunt, taking the brunt of the blow and toppling beneath a large mass—a man. The intruder turned my way, eyes the color of midnight ink. Not a man. A demon.

Forearm braced behind Jax's neck to keep him down, it delivered a series of harsh blows. "Take her outside," the demon snarled.

I spun to see that a second demon had appeared and stepped between Jax and me. Its eyes—narrow, soulless black orbs—traveled over my body, from tip to toe, hungry and assessing. "Submit, or spend an eternity in agony," it said.

I had no idea what the hell it was talking about and didn't care. I ducked as it made a swipe in my direction, then spun away, losing my bearings for a moment. I'd managed to avoid it, but the demon wasn't giving up. Another attempt and its hands wrapped like a vise around my arm and dragged me close. Putrid breath wafted around me.

"Sammy!" Jax yelled. He pushed off the floor, throwing the other demon off balance. But it recovered quickly, and just as he got to his feet, it charged. They both went down again.

"He will not stop us from taking you," growled the demon attached to my arm. Its grip bit into my skin, bringing involuntary tears to my eyes. If it squeezed much harder, my arm was likely to pop off.

"News for you, asshole." I struggled—in vain—and it tightened its grip. "You're not taking me anyplace." I had no clue why I was suddenly catnip to these things, but I had no intention of *submitting* to a damn thing.

"I killed a Son of Cain a hundred years ago." The thing faced me and with a wicked sneer. "They break as easily as humans. You have no choice."

Anger welled up inside me, and even though I knew it was pointless, I lashed out with my free hand, punching and clawing at whatever I could hit. One of my flailing blows caught it in the eye. The demon cursed and stumbled back, releasing my arm, and I tore across the room.

As I neared him, Jax was climbing to his feet again.

He ducked, missing what looked like a powerful blow by inches, and pivoted, bringing both fists upward. The motion connected with the underside of the enemy's jaw.

He readied, probably expecting it to come at him again, but it didn't. It recovered and charged me instead. Jax bolted forward, but the demon was closer.

Everything went silent and the entire room slowed. A single blow. I felt the impact, felt my feet actually leaving the floor, then my body shot sideways and hit the wall with brutal force. Everything grew hazy. A sound split the air, a horrible noise that could have scared the devil. It shook the walls and rattled the fixtures, and when my vision cleared, I got chills when I spied the source.

It'd come from Jax.

He was on the demon that threw me in an instant. Everything was tearing flesh and splatters of gore. Eerie sounds of destruction followed on the heels of that agonized howl. The thing put up a fight, but was no match for his unadulterated rage. When he was done there was nothing left. The demon was a pile of unrecognizable pulp.

Satisfied, Jax whirled on the next one. It watched me with a hungry gleam and an excited shiver. I scooted backward as the demon lunged, and Jax charged. They crashed to the ground, narrowly missing me as I stumbled up and dove behind the couch for cover.

But the demon wasn't interested in Jax. It wanted me. Badly. Bucking Jax off, it made another attempt to grab me, launching itself over the couch and latching on to a handful of my hair. It jerked back hard, and I couldn't help it. I screamed.

"It belongs to us," the thing said with a growl, giving another, brutal yank. I had no choice other than to follow the momentum, rising to my feet as tears stung my eyes.

"*She* belongs to me," Jax roared. There was a rush of air, and a half second later the pressure at my temple disappeared.

He grasped the demon's head on either side and twisted. One good snap and its hands fell slack as it crumpled to the floor. Jax opened his mouth, but something charged between us, knocking us apart.

"*Death* belongs to you, traitor." A new demon barreled into the fray, snarling at Jax. Jesus. These things just kept coming.

It traded blows with him halfway across the room. Jax threw his whole body forward, forehead crashing into the demon's with a resounding crack. It stumbled back, and he followed through with a blow to the side of its head, then another one, even more brutal than the first, to its throat. But just as Jax was about to deliver the deathblow, something exploded through the large picture window in the dining room.

A blur streaked across the room. I cried out a warning—it was headed for Jax—but it moved too fast. It collided with him and the other demon and knocked them apart. The newcomer pivoted and turned on Jax's attacker. "We are not here to harm our Lord," it growled.

The first one made a sound deep in its throat but backed away. Seemingly satisfied, the newcomer stood, glaring at Jax, then turned to me.

"Don't even think about it," Jax warned.

Its gaze lingered on me for a moment longer, lips twisted and teeth bared, before it relaxed and switched its focus to Jax. "Fear not, Lord Azirak. We have dispatched the enemy and mean you no harm."

"Could have fooled me," I mumbled. The place was a mess. Broken furniture and spattered gore decorated a large part of the room. And the smell? It was like a thousand piles of roadkill.

The demon's gaze swiveled back to me. "We understand now why Lord Azirak keeps you, but…" It growled and came another step closer. "Maintain your distance. Malphi will not tolerate your stink on him."

"Malphi…" Jax tensed. "Is that who sent you? Those two—"

"Were of Zenak's clan. I apologize for not arriving sooner." The demon's eyebrows disappeared beneath shaggy bangs. Wearing a Yankee's cap and worn blue jeans, he looked like a college kid ready for the weekend. "As for Malphi…do you remember, my lord?"

I didn't need the link to know Jax was two steps away from ramming his fist down the demon's throat. All that *my lord* crap.

Wait…

My lord crap? Only members of Azi's clan referred to Jax that way. But it'd mentioned Malphi. Oh my God… Malphi was part of Azi's clan?

"I know the name. That's all," Jax said, deceptively calm. I had no clue how he held it together. His rage simmered just beneath the surface. I could taste it through the link, a potent, coppery tang that coated the back of my throat.

"The name…" the demon repeated. If I didn't know better, I would have said it looked disappointed. There was the slightest twitch of its lip and a subtle slump of the shoulders. "No matter. Malphi knows you—and has asked me to deliver a message."

"What kind of message?"

It turned to me, eerie black eyes boring straight into mine. "Agree to be claimed, or be destroyed."

Jax snorted. The spark of fury still lingered in his eyes, but there was also excitement. "You first." He grabbed the demon's head between his hands and twisted hard. Apparently the fact that it'd been one of Azi's demons wasn't an issue. It fell to the floor in a lifeless heap. With a nod to the last remaining demon, he jabbed a finger at me and said, "Report back to Malphi. Whatever it is you want with Sam, forget it. It's never going to happen."

With one final snap of its teeth, the demon slipped through the broken window.

"You okay?"

The cuff on my wrist tightened, and a feeling of dread bubbled deep in the pit of my stomach. In the basement back at the Viking, the guy had insisted I *submit*. The demon said the same thing a few minutes ago. What the hell was going on? "Claimed? What was he talking about?"

"I dunno, Sammy. But I bet Heckle has a clue." Jax watched me with an odd expression. Almost as if he expected me to crack. "We have to find him."

"Agreed," I responded. "But first we should clean up."

He was covered in blood. Everything was covered in blood, actually. Rick's previously beige striped couch was coated in carnage, as were the curtains and carpet. The coffee table was smashed to pieces and scattered around the room. It was pure destruction...which I was becoming strangely used to. Six months ago something like this would have freaked me out. Now it was just another day. There was a strange sense of familiarity in it all and that scared the crap out of me.

As I shook my arm, Jax looked from the cuff to me. The doorbell rang and he threw up his hands. "I call bullshit here... It's like two in the morning—who the hell could be out there?"

"Well, at least we know it's not a demon. They're far too rude to ring the bell."

He snorted. "Never know."

"There really is no such thing as a break, is there?" I said, crossing the room to the door. I had the urge to rub the inside of my wrist but resisted, figuring it would only make him antsier. When I pulled back the curtains, I groaned. There on the step was the worst possible visitor. A demon might have actually been preferable. It was our next door neighbor—my Aunt Kelly. "Our messy living room and my spanking new demon jewelry isn't our only problem..."

Chapter Five

"Not good..." Sam yanked the curtains back into place and spun around. The link between us surged to life, a fresh wave of panic flooding through it.

I frowned. The last thing we needed with a house full of corpses was an uninvited visitor. "There was a lot of noise. Did someone call the cops?"

"It's Kelly!" she said, stomping her foot. "*Kelly* is standing on the front porch."

Perfect fucking timing, as usual. I scanned the living room. The place looked like the set of a high budget slasher flick, blood and bodies strewn all over. "Get rid of her," I snapped. We didn't need Sam's nosey aunt poking around right now. Or ever. She didn't know about me and I intended to keep it that way.

Sam took a deep breath and opened the door a crack. "Kelly," she said, voice ringing with forced cheerfulness. Kelly should have been able to see through it. She'd raised Sam, after all. But she was as clueless now as she had been when we were young. "It's after midnight. Are you okay?"

"I heard loud noises." The elder Merrick tried to push into the house, but Sam blocked her.

"Noises? What kind of noises?" When Kelly found out Sam moved from her apartment and in with me, her head exploded. There was yelling and screaming and large amounts of dramatic bullshit. She'd never been a fan, always pushing Sam toward my brother Chase who, ironically, was the real bad seed. Usually I never missed an opportunity to rub our living situation in her face, but I kept quiet now. "I haven't heard any noises."

Kelly tried to push past her again. "Don't play games with me, Samantha. I know what I heard. Things falling and breaking. Clanking and clattering. It sounded like a war over here."

"Clanking and clattering," Sam repeated, nodding her head.

"Is he manipulating you?" Kelly dropped her voice. I couldn't see around Sam, but I'd bet she was squinting. The damn woman loved to squint. "Making you pay your rent in the form of *favors*?"

Sam nearly choked, and I snorted. "Is he...favors? Are you *insane*? Where do you come up with this shit?"

A gasp. "Language, Samantha!" She paused, then let go of an overly dramatic sigh. "I told you he was trouble. I warned you—"

"Sex!" Sam blurted out. "We were having sex. Wild, crazy, animal-like sex."

I would have given both nuts to see Kelly's face.

"Yep," Sam continued, running with it. She shifted her body to block the possibility of even a pinhole view. "It got a little intense. He's into some kinky stuff. You should see his—"

Kelly gasped again, and a moment later I heard her

footsteps as she power-walked away.

"Thank God," Sam said, closing the door. She turned back to me, cringing at the mess. "So what now?"

I folded my arms and leaned back against a clean spot on the wall. "You didn't finish your conversation with Kelly. See my *what*, exactly?"

"Your ego," Sam fired back. "So damn big it barely fits in the door." She wiggled her hand. "Can we focus here?"

"Okay," I said, giving up and stepping away from the wall. The ease with which she was taking all this worried me. Sam was a tough cookie, but she seemed unfazed by the carnage. Strangely detached. "We need to find out what the hell that thing is on your wrist. I don't love the idea, but if Heckle can't remove it, we might have to hunt this Malphi down…"

"Agreed." She nodded and stuffed both hands into her pockets, avoiding my gaze. "But, mess first. Let's focus on that. Okay? We can't risk someone finding bloody corpses in your living room."

I studied her. The colors dancing above her head were a strange mix, a swirl of conflicting hues. Sam was usually fairly even. Mad, sad, happy. Her emotions were always clear. Now though, she seemed muddled, all over the radar, despite her eerily calm demeanor. "Are you okay?"

Her eyes darted from me to her wrist, then back again. She smiled, but it was forced. "Totally okay."

I nodded. What else could I do? She'd just lied to me.

I tried again to get hold of Heckle, but he was still conveniently unreachable. Since we lived in a semi-rural, developed area, carting corpses out to the car wouldn't go unnoticed—especially since Kelly was probably camped out at her bedroom window with binoculars glued to her face.

We only had one choice.

"Knock, knock," a sultry voice said from the back door.

Sadie Gray was a witch Heckle had referred us to a few months ago, but our connection was complicated. Hell, all my relationships were complicated. She limped through the door, and when she entered the room, Sam gasped. I understood why. Sadie looked almost as bad as the living room. Bruises covered her face, and a nasty gash—one that started at the right corner of her lip and disappeared behind her ear—seeped blood.

She noticed us staring and waggled her fingers in my direction. "Oh, this? I'd assumed you pissed someone off, or possibly took up cage fighting as a hobby."

Despite my contempt for the witch, a ripple of guilt washed over me. I'd forgotten about the effects of our link. "Shit."

In order to help thwart the control Chase had over Sam, Sadie offered me a special stone that had allowed Sam enough leeway for her to get away. But not without the witch demanding something in return. For reasons we still hadn't figured out, she'd forced me to link us. Unfortunately, unlike the one Sam forged, a demonic link was mainly beneficial to the demon. If I was harmed, Sadie was the one who took most of the damage. I'd warned her, but she hadn't cared.

"Aww," Sadie said, winking. "Don't go worrying about little ol' me."

"I wasn't," I said. "Just surprised. You asked for this, Sadie. Don't expect me to feel sorry for you."

She shrugged, not the least put off—which only made the whole thing more suspicious. Sadie had her reasons for wanting the link. I hadn't trusted her then, and I sure as hell didn't trust her now, but what was done was done. "Wouldn't dream of it, handsome. So, why the summons?"

Sam shifted from foot to foot in the doorway. The look

of disdain in her eyes was unmistakable—not that I blamed her. Sadie had made her desire for something more from our relationship crystal clear, and even though Sam knew I had zero interest, she still hated the witch.

"I need you to ward the house," I said, wasting no time. She'd made her bed and now she'd have to bleed in it.

I'd dragged the bodies—what was left of them—into the corner of the dining room and covered them with a tarp while Sam pulled down the curtains and replaced them with clean ones, but the place was still a mess.

"Ward the house?" Sadie repeated, taking another unsteady step inside the room. "Exactly what do you mean?" She examined the stains on the floor, eyebrows rising slightly. "I assume this little mess means you were attacked?"

"I mean magic," I said, ignoring her question. "Some kind of protection spell. Strongest you have."

Sadie stepped over to one of the dark spots on the carpet and nudged it with the toe of her shoe. "Protection against what?"

"Demons." I pulled back the tarp covering the corpses.

If Sadie was surprised or sickened, she didn't show it. She studied the pile of bodies with nothing more than clinical interest, then shrugged. "Well, warding might be a problem."

"Problem? Why?" I snapped. Azi's patience—and mine with it—was wearing thin.

Sadie flicked a red-tipped finger in my direction. "Because *you're* technically a demon?"

Shit. I hadn't thought about that.

"Obviously it matters?" Sam asked tightly. A wave of contempt rushed through the link.

"It does unless he plans on moving out." Sadie pulled the tarp back over the bodies and placed both hands on her hips. She glared at Sam. "If I ward it against demons, Jax won't be able to come in. So, unless you'd like him to move in with me…"

"Pass." The turbulence in her voice went right through me. She pulled her hair back into a tail, eyes following the witch wherever she went. "If you can't ward the place, then what do we do?"

Sadie shrugged. "Not a thing. Not here, anyway."

"If there's no way to keep them out, then we can't stay." I turned away. The red haze bleeding into the air trailed behind Sam as she moved, like a snake waiting to strike. If Sadie wasn't careful, she was going to pounce. Azi shifted, excited. The prospect of violence was even more alluring than her anger. "Not willing to risk it."

For a minute, I was sure she'd argue. She knew damn well the *it* I didn't want to risk was her. Reluctantly though, she sighed and held up her wrist. The metal bracelet glinted in the light. "What about this? Can you do anything about it?"

An expression of pure horror slipped across Sadie's face. She grabbed Sam's wrist and wrenched her arm closer, nearly pulling her over. "Where did you get this?"

"Why?" I was beside them in an instant. The markings on the cuff gave a flash. "Do you know what it is?"

"It's a Fakori Cuff," Sadie said. "Known in darker circles as a demon's cuff."

Sam looked like she was about to deck the witch, so I stepped between them. If there was a chance she could remove the thing, then it was best not to piss her off.

"What do you know about it?" I repeated.

Sadie sighed. "Fakori was said to be an alchemist, having imbued a number of bracelets with powerful curses of demonic nature."

"Curses of demonic nature?" Sam asked. She looked a little pale. "What does that mean?"

"Nothing good. Each cuff does something different." Sadie's eyes were trained on Sam, full of awe. "That thing is humming." She took Sam's hand again and ran her pointer finger along the underside of her wrist. Closing her eyes, her lips began to move. Chanting. Every few seconds, her brow furrowed, like she was concentrating extra hard.

After a moment, Sam gasped and tried to pull away, but Sadie wouldn't let go. Her grip tightened, knuckles going white as the symbols along the metal glowed bright red. A second later, the witch let out a scream and shot backward across the room.

"What did you do?" I asked, going to help her off the floor.

Sadie grimaced as she struggled to her feet. "Not even going to ask if I'm okay?"

"Nope." I didn't have time for her dramatics. When she'd bargained for the link between us, she'd essentially forced me to do something against my will, taking advantage of our bad situation. I wasn't about to pity her for it. "Don't care."

She bristled, then shrugged it off. "Honesty. That's sexy."

Sam made a fist again then flexed her fingers. "I'm guessing the unplanned display of acrobatics means you can't take this thing off."

"That thing isn't coming off unless the person who put it there takes it off." Sadie sank onto the couch—the end not covered in blood splatter—wincing with every move. "It might help to tell me where you got it."

"Someone bad," I said.

She thought about it for a minute before flashing Sam a grin. With a waggle of her fingers in my direction, she said, "Well then, in my professional opinion, you're well and truly fucked."

I was on my feet and dragging her off the couch by the front of her shirt in a half beat of her heart. "You're going to fix this," I snarled.

As unflappable as ever, Sadie simply shook her head.

"Sorry, baby. There's nothing I can do. Only the one who put it on her can remove it. Dead or alive."

"Dead or alive?" Sam's colors swirled, still muddied and thick.

"There's a rumor that if a person places a demon cuff, its power is tied to them. If you kill them, it might release Sam as well. In the meantime, I *might* be able to track it."

"Track it?" Sam was fidgeting, clenching her hands and digging her fingers into her palms. She glared at Sadie. The look made me think she was having a flash of her own. Possibly of beating the witch to a bloody pulp.

"All magic leaves a trace—even alchemy. The *bad person* who put it there may not be an alchemist, but the power will leave its mark. A good witch"—she winked—"and I *am* good—can possibly track the source. Maybe you can use your own special brand of *persuasion* to get them to remove it."

She made a show of straightening her shirt then turned back to the tarp. With a snap of her fingers, the whole pile disappeared, along with the remaining mess in the room. The couch and carpet were spotless, and the splatters decorating the walls and the ceiling were gone. Even the glass was back in place. I did my best to hide my surprise. I hadn't dealt with other witches, but if they were all as powerful as Sadie, they could give the demons a run for their money.

I doubted there was anything I could do to *persuade* Chase to remove the cuff. Other than doing what he wanted, anyway. But having her track him down would provide a failsafe. I'd kill him if I had to. Fuck the rest of the world. Let hell come. Sam was all that mattered to me. "Do it."

"I'll work my magic." She limped toward the door and paused with her hand on the knob. "No promises though. In the meantime, you should probably lay low. Fakori cuffs, whatever their individual purposes are, are dangerous."

S am insisted that Sadie ward Kelly's house before leaving. I wouldn't admit it, but it was a good idea. Sam had gone over, introduced her as a friend, and kept her aunt busy while Sadie did what she needed to. After that, we'd each packed a bag and gotten in Rick's old car. It was almost nine in the morning when we pulled up outside the Inferno.

I parked in front of the bar and killed the engine. Sam hadn't said a word since we'd left the house. She'd spent the entire drive staring down at her wrist. The demon got frustrated when she was upset. Sometimes downright violent. I felt it welling up and clenched my fists tight to keep from smashing them against the dashboard.

"We'll figure this out." I unfastened the seat belt and got out of the car as she did, hurrying to the door of the bar. When I pulled on the handle, it didn't open. The place was dark.

"Not a good sign." Sam cupped her hands against the glass to peer inside. The smallest flutter of gray rose from her shoulders, sticking out against the still swirling muck of her emotions. "He's always here."

"Well, he's not right now." No need to upset her further by telling her I'd already tried the Inferno on the way home last night. Or that Heckle still hadn't returned the messages I'd left, and his cell phone voicemail was now full. I tugged her away from the building. "Let's go. I don't want to stand out in the open."

"Hey there," someone said as we started walking back to the car.

I turned. The man was tall, with a lean but sturdy build and odd green eyes. The expression on his face bothered me. It was too warm. Eager, almost. But that wasn't what put Azi on alert. Every human had colors. Happy, sad, horny, or pissed—they were always there, even if only as the faintest waves rising to tint the air around their shoulders. This guy? There was nothing. Not a wisp in sight. He smelled wrong, too, and I couldn't peg it. Not a demon. Not human. A creature I'd never seen before. "Not interested," I said, taking Sam's hand and sidestepping him.

"You here to see Heckle?" the guy called.

I had every intention of getting into the car and moving on, but Sam stopped and turned. "You know where he is?"

The guy smiled at her. Beamed like the fucking sun. It made me want to put my fist through the back of his head. "He's tied up at the moment, but I know where he is. I can take you if you'd like."

Sam looked from him to me, expression hopeful, and I snorted. "No," I said to her, teetering on the edge of anger. The sun was just cresting the buildings, and the Monday morning traffic was starting to increase.

"We need to find him," she said, leaning close. A surge of gray rolled off her.

I looked from her to the guy. Still no sign of emotion. "What are you?" I asked, maneuvering myself between him and Sam. "'Cause you sure as shit ain't human."

The guy laughed. Not annoyed or defensive. Amused. The fucker thought it was funny. "No, I'm definitely not a human." He looked back toward the Inferno and laughed. "I doubt there are many humans who know Heckle personally."

"That didn't answer his question," Sam said.

Finally she was getting the picture.

"You truly don't know?" he asked, taking a step toward us. Eyes on mine, he smiled.

"Not a human." Sam tilted her head. "You don't look like the Easter Bunny. So, what *are* you?"

"An interested party," he replied, that same twisted smile on his face. Azi shifted, and a flash hit me like a sucker punch to the nuts—two hulking forms, their shadows looming against an unfamiliar battlefield.

"His eyes," Sam said with a gasp.

Her voice pulled me from the vision. The man's eyes were black as night. "A demon," I whispered, stunned. I inhaled, breathing in my surroundings. Sewage. Old garbage. Car exhaust. Sam. That was all. Not right. That couldn't be right. Demons had a scent. They had colors. It was unmistakable and impossible to hide.

I took Sam's hand and tugged her close. The thing's gaze followed, staying locked on our intertwined fingers. It laughed again, but it was different. Sharp and dangerous. Predatory.

It reminded me...of me.

"You got me. I'm a demon." It motioned over its shoulder to a dark SUV parked a few storefronts down. "I can take you where you need to go."

Was it that fucking stupid? To think we'd just get in the truck?

It laughed. "Do you not recognize me, Azirak?" Arms folding across its chest, the demon pinned me with a pitying gaze.

"I'm not Azirak," I responded coolly.

"Aren't you?" It leaned closer, inhaling deeply. A smile split the thing's lips. "I know you feel it. The power inside you, straining against the seams of that pathetic human body. The desire to be reunited with your clan." It leaned back, grin widening into something close to madness. "What if I uttered the name...*Malphi*? Would your body not react?"

I returned the thing's smug grin with one of my own then flipped it off.

Or, that's what I wanted to do. Unfortunately, at the mention of Malphi, a jolt raced through my system, seizing every limb. My feet turned leaden and my heart thundered against my ribs. It was like I'd been dipped in ice water then dropped into boiling lava. Every nerve ending was humming and my body alive.

"What's wrong, *Jax*?" the demon drawled.

Sam watched me, her colors swirling a chaotic black and gray. "Jax?"

"I'm fine," I managed. "And to answer your question, yes. My body did react—with the urge to rip Malphi apart one piece at a time."

The thing's grin widened knowingly, and it bared its teeth. "You lie. You feel their connection."

"Whatever Malphi is to Azirak, it means nothing to me." I shoved the demon hard in the chest. "But don't relay the message, man. I'll do it right before I kill the bastard."

I turned to walk away, but it grabbed my arm and held tight.

"Unless you have an army waiting in the shadows, I suggest you remove your hand and step aside." What I really wanted was to shred it limb from limb, but Harlow was starting to wake. There were people on the street, and odds were good someone would notice a bloody fight to the death. The police chief wasn't a fan of mine. I'd bet good money he'd be thrilled to have an excuse to throw me behind bars and toss away the key.

It let go and stepped away. "You are mistaken, Lord Azirak. I'm not here to fight. Only to see if you've come to a decision." Its eyes fell to the demon cuff around Sam's wrist. It looked different than before. Tighter.

"Decision?" I asked.

"About the girl."

Malphi.

It gestured toward Sam. "About the Pure."

"Pure?" I maneuvered myself in front of her.

Its eyes were hungry, watching Sam like she was the ultimate feast. "You don't know the power you have control of. It is that reason alone that your betrayal of the clan will be forgiven. Come back to your family. Bring the Pure and claim her."

"No one has control over me," Sam snapped. She pushed her way around me, glaring at the demon.

It only laughed. Turning, it started to walk away, calling over its shoulder, "Your kind was born to be controlled."

Chapter Six

Your kind was born to be controlled.

The demon's words lingered long after he'd left the alley—which felt like a trap. He pops in, chats us up, then leaves? No. Something was definitely up. Demons weren't known for their restraint.

Over the last month, I'd grown increasingly nervous about the things I didn't know. The things Heckle *refused* to tell me. How had I been able to create the link between Jax and me, and why was I so damn special? The cuff around my wrist gave a squeeze and my breath caught. I passed *nervous* and rolled right into panic.

"We'll figure it out," Jax said. He didn't sound convinced, though. He didn't look it, either. His left eyebrow kept twitching, and every few minutes he'd knead the fingers of his right fist into his palm. I felt his unease as though it was my own.

"*My kind.*" I repeated what the demon said, tearing my

gaze away from the cuff. Every once in a while the symbols on the surface would pulsate, and the thing would tighten. "What *kind* is that?"

"We'll figure it out," he said again, looking left, then right. He made a grab for my arm, but I sidestepped him, and he sighed. "We really need to get off the street."

"And go where?" The last few months had been a rollercoaster of surreal. I'd died, been controlled, used as leverage, and ultimately had my life turned inside out. But I'd come back from it, stronger and more determined to set things right for Jax and me so that we'd have the future we deserved. Not once during all of it did I consider the possibility of failure. Of surrender. That wasn't me. I didn't quit. Jax joked that my stubbornness was borderline terminal. Yet in that moment the weight of despair and worry was stronger than anything I'd ever experienced. We would fail. We had to. There was no scenario in which I came out on top—or alive. I held up my wrist. "I'm not sure there's a way around this."

"There is," he insisted. I wasn't sure if he was trying to convince me, or himself. "We know that Malphi wants Azirak back in the fold. I can use that."

"Even if we find Malphi, I don't think killing it will be as easy as your run of the mill demon. If it were that simple, then Chase would do it himself." I shook my head. He needed to hear it. To understand and accept things. Hopeless. This was all hopeless. "I'm going to die, Jax." And this time it would be permanent.

"What the fuck is wrong with you?" He slammed his hand against the hood of Rick's car, eyes drifting downward to the cuff. "Since when did you jump the doom and gloom train?"

"You need to understand—"

"Enough of this shit," he roared. With a jab of his finger he said, "You better get your damn head straight, Sammy. Because this isn't you."

As if in response, the skin beneath the cuff tingled, giving way to a spike of pain. I gritted my teeth and held my breath. There was no point in letting Jax know.

"Even if you manage to do what he asked, there's no guarantee Chase will hold up his end of the deal. Plus, we don't have all the facts. He can't be trusted. For all we know, this is a trap. Maybe killing Malphi will make things worse somehow."

Jax took my hand and brushed his thumb over top of the cuff. The metal warmed, sending a pulse of heat deep into my skin. "Fine," he said with a sharp nod. "You want facts? Then let's get them."

Jax had me drive while he called Sadie. The conversation lasted longer than I'd expected, and he'd been quiet since hanging up. I didn't need the link between us to tell me something was wrong.

"You ever gonna tell me what she said?" I moved into the right lane to let the guy behind me pass. He was driving too close, slowly crawling up our ass, and I was tempted to slam the brakes. God. I was so damn uneven all of a sudden. Not nuclear like Jax could be, but more volatile than normal. Either he was starting to rub off on me, or the stress of all this was causing me to lose my mind. One minute I felt like a time bomb, as if one spark would ignite me past the point of rationality. The next I felt as though life wasn't worth living. It was making me dizzy.

"We need to hurry," he said quietly.

I didn't disagree with him, but we didn't have any clue how to remove the cuff other than doing what Chase asked and hoping he kept his word. "Short of cutting off my arm or taking out this Malphi guy, I'm not sure what to do."

No response.

"This is insane," I said with a sigh. "Will you please talk to me? What did Sadie say?"

"Pull over." The chill in his voice froze the air in my lungs. "Jax?"

"Pull over!" The words boomed through the small space. I slammed the brake and cut the wheel, bringing the car to a jerky stop in the gravel on the side of the road.

"It needs to come off, Sammy. It needs to come off now," he said, back to that quiet-yet-furious voice. He punched a fist against the roof of the car, ripping the fabric and denting the metal upward.

"Okay," I said, twisting in the seat. "It's okay. *I'm* okay. Do you need to fee—"

"You're not hearing me!" he roared. "Don't you see it?"

I jumped and took a deep breath. His eyes were rimmed with black, and every inch of him screamed tension. "See what? What did Sadie say?"

"The longer that cuff is on, the more damage it does," he replied.

I shook my head. He was borderline, at that point where slipping over the edge would take nothing more than the shifting of the breeze. If what he felt through the link was anything remotely close to what I felt, he'd know every word I said was bullshit. "We have time."

He raised his head, gaze meeting mine, and it was hard not to move away. There was anger in his eyes. Anger that, for the first time I could remember, was obviously directed at me.

"That thing is affecting you," he said, his tone as close to demonic as I'd ever heard. The black ring around his irises grew a little wider.

"It's not—"

"Don't!" he bellowed, and I jumped. The entire car shook at the sound of his voice as the darkness took over.

His eyes changed, becoming pools of midnight. "Don't tell me it's nothing. Don't tell me you're fine. I can feel it." His fist crashed against the dash. At this rate he was going to take the car apart before we got where we were going. "Don't you think I can fucking *feel* it? See it? Christ, Sammy. You're not right."

"What do you mean, not right?"

"The way you were pushing me back at the house, and how you were looking at Sadie. Fucking hell. You just got finished telling me that I had to *deal with* the fact that you were going to die! Even your colors are wrong. They've been that way since Chase slapped that cuff on you."

I'd been thinking it, but hearing him say it out loud felt like a tsunami rolling over my head. It meant it wasn't just my overactive imagination.

"We don't know anything yet," I said, trying to reason with him. I realized, though, his anger was totally justified. I sucked in a breath. "Yes. I feel…different."

I blinked, and suddenly he was touching me, hands gripping either side of my face with a savage ferocity that gave me chills. "I can't have you, but I won't lose you."

Gently I laid my hands over his and let my head fall forward until our foreheads touched. He was so close. So warm. Jax had been my comfort in times of stress and heartbreak when I was younger. I needed that now. To feel safe. To feel *something*. All I would have to do to taste him was tilt my head…

"You were looking for me?"

I jumped. Lounging across the backseat was Heckle, dressed in a ski jacket and boots, and holding a ski pole.

"Where the fuck have you been?" Jax snapped.

Heckle, as usual, was unaffected. "I wasn't aware that I needed to report to you when I went out of town." His gaze swung in my direction. His eyebrows rose slightly, and his lips melted into a grim line. "Is there a shortage of space in the car?"

I pulled away guiltily.

"We didn't do anything," Jax said tightly.

Heckle kept his eyes on mine. "But you were going to—which is part of the reason I'm here."

This was nothing compared to what we'd been doing in the basement at the Viking. Or in my room. He couldn't have chosen *then* to pop in?

I'll admit it. The guy creeped me out sometimes—and not because I knew who he really was.

My aunt Kelly raised me after my parents died, and she'd never been an overly religious woman. We went to church on the holidays. Your typical fair-weather Catholics. But I knew the story of Cain and Abel. Cain killed his brother Abel out of jealousy, bringing darkness to the world. What the Church doesn't tell you is that after his untimely death, Abel went on to bigger and better things.

Oh, and he'd changed his name.

To Bel Heckle.

Heckle waggled a finger between Jax and me, narrowing his eyes. "Have you figured out how to break the link?"

"No," I said, trying hard to keep my tone even. Heckle might play the part of the wise-cracking, quirky bartender at the Inferno, but I'd seen the power he could control with a simple snap of his fingers. I didn't even want to think about what he could do to a smart-mouthed girl who was pissy because she and her boyfriend couldn't get freaky. "I'm working on it."

Ever since I'd unknowingly linked Jax and me, Heckle had been on my ass about breaking it. He hadn't told me why, or more importantly, *how*, but never failed to harp on it every chance he got.

"Well, work harder. You—" He leaned over the seat and

seized my hand. His eyes widened. "Why are you wearing a Fakori cuff?"

"A gift from my brother," Jax said coolly.

His grip around my wrist tightened, and I bit back a yelp. "Chase is here?"

"He came to the Viking last night." I yanked my hand from his, cradling it to my chest protectively. "Gave us an ultimatum."

"What kind of ultimatum?"

"Apparently there's a big bad demon trolling the town. He said if we took it down, he would remove the cuff." I peered at Jax from the corner of my eye. "He said something else, too."

I hesitated, and Heckle tapped his finger against the seat. "Well?"

"He told us you owed us, Heckle. What was he talking about?"

Heckle didn't say anything. He was still staring at the cuff.

"Well?" Jax prompted. His patience was waning and I didn't blame him.

Nothing.

"Heckle?" I tried, doing my best to keep the irritation from my voice.

"What demon did Chase tell you to kill?"

"A demon called Malphi," Jax responded. "Any idea why?"

More silence. I wasn't sure if it scared me or made me angrier. Considering the simmering vibes I was getting from Jax through the link, I was leaning toward pissed. "What's a Pure?"

If I hadn't been staring right at him, I would have missed it. A flash of surprise, there and gone, in his eyes.

"You have ten seconds to start answering questions." There was ice in Jax's voice, and if the twitching fingers and tense set of his jaw were any indication, he was fast approaching the point of no return. "Tell me how to get this thing off her."

"You can't." Heckle finally lifted his gaze from the cuff and fixed his attention on me. "If Chase put it there, I'm fairly certain he's the only one who can remove it. Personally, or by his death. Since killing him isn't an option, you have one choice. Do as he says."

"Because Chase is a man of his word, right?" I couldn't believe I was hearing this. "Do either of you really believe he's going to remove this thing if we hold up our end of the deal? This is a trap!"

Heckle sighed. "Yes. I imagine that it is."

Jax took a deep breath and closed his eyes for a moment. When he opened them, they were rimmed with black. "Enough of the cryptic bullshit."

I grabbed his hand as he reached for Heckle. "Please. You have to give us something." Desperation found its way into my voice, and I dropped Jax's hand in favor of Heckle's. Squeezing tight, I said, "He told us you owed us. If that's even a tiny bit true, then help us. Please."

He pulled away, and with a sigh said, "Maintaining a balance between good and evil is not an easy task. There are millions of variables, and, of course, free will to contend with. I try my hardest, but the scales have been tipped, this time by my own foolish choices. I am truly sorry, Sam."

"Sorry?" Jax slammed his hand against the dashboard. "Sorry about what? What are you not telling us?"

"When I agreed to bring you back after dying in order to sever the link with Chase, I didn't know what would happen."

An arctic chill invaded the car. I shivered. His words felt like the barrel of a gun, pointed right between my eyes. Fully loaded, safety off, and an itching finger caressing the trigger. "That *what* would happen?"

"I knew what you were. A Pure. I knew the rules—that

once a Pure's soul is separated from the body, its power becomes active. Claimable by anyone able to grasp their power. What I didn't know was the ramifications of returning that soul to a body. I thought you would return to an inactive state, but you retained the power you gained in death. In fact it made you stronger and, much worse, visible to anyone with a supernatural eye." He turned to Jax. "You must see it when you look at her. That she has sort of a glow?"

Jax turned his gaze on me. Squinting, he shrugged. "She's always had a sort of glow. Nothing looks different to me."

"Hmmm. I don't understand that, but in truth, it's not important." Heckle's lips pressed in a firm line and, with his eyes cast downward, he sighed. "I'm truly sorry, Sam. I've painted a permanent neon target on your head."

Chapter Seven

"A target," Sam repeated, shifting in the seat. I could taste her mounting anger—not fear of the danger she was in but rage, tangible fury over Heckle's admission. "A target for who?"

"For everyone," he replied. "Your kind is hidden for good reason, and I have jeopardized things."

"Malphi knows about Sam," I said, a small—very small— bit of last night's chaos coming together. "Some of its demons came last night to deliver a message. It wants me to return to the clan with Sam."

"Malphi is a force to be reckoned with. A major player. If it knows Sam is a Pure, it will stop at nothing to possess her. If you were to remove it from the playing field—"

"So you're saying Chase is telling the truth?" I grimaced. "That we have no choice but do what he wants, because Malphi is a threat?"

"Technically. Unfortunately, there are complications."

"Aren't there always?" Sam mumbled. "What are we talking about now?"

"The demon cuff itself is one snag—a rather brilliant one at that. If you are unable to kill Malphi before the cuff reaches the end of its cycle, I have no doubt that Chase will use it as a bargaining chip."

"Meaning?" Sam asked.

"My guess is that he'll offer to remove the cuff in exchange for claiming you."

"Because she's a Pure," I said. I saw Sam from the corner of my eye. She was tapping her foot and kneading both fists until the knuckles went white.

"Yes," Heckle confirmed.

"Claiming me... What *exactly* does that mean?" Her voice was even, but her eyes... There was a flash of emptiness. How long would it be until she lost herself completely?

Heckle's response was silence, and Sam had obviously reached her limit. A flash of red stood out against the haze. She jabbed the seat belt release and kicked open the driver's side door, stomping past the gravel and into the grass. "I want answers," she demanded. "I want to know what the fuck I am! Am I even human?"

A car passed, kicking up a blast of wind, and her hair flew in all directions, giving her a wild, feral look. Her emotions were charged, the smoke churning like a tornado around her entire body. The scent it gave off was heady. It enticed Azi closer to the surface, making the demon unsettled and hungry.

I pushed through the passenger's side door and rounded the car, the sight of her stopping me in my tracks. Sam was no church mouse, but the level of rage that bled into the air was unlike her.

It was like me.

"I promise you, Sam," Heckle said, his voice soothing as he extracted himself from the backseat. "You are one hundred percent human. However, right now I need you to calm yourself."

"I'm human? That tells me absolutely nothing," she spat, and in a move that left me stunned, flew at him. Heckle didn't try to move. She crashed into him with impressive force, knocking them back against the car. "I want answers!"

"Some people are born different," he replied, speaking with complete calm. She had him pinned to the hood, but he made no move to dislodge her. "Special. The kind of special you are is rare. It's valuable."

She grabbed a handful of his jacket and shook. "Valuable? To who?"

"Everyone," was Heckle's reply.

"But why?"

"As you already know, some acts leave a hideous stain on the souls of our offspring, as with the Tainted. Other acts— good ones—cleanse them. They become purified." Heckle frowned. He gently placed his hands over top of Sam's and pried them loose. "A Pure is a rare thing. Acts of true benevolence are not something you see often, especially in this day and age."

The swirling, muddied miasma around Sam swallowed some of the red. She let go of him and backed away. "So, I'm the opposite of Jax?"

"In a manner of speaking, yes." He nodded. "As with the Tainted, the purified piece of the soul gets passed from parent to child, possibly going for centuries, depending on the act that initiated it. You have no idea how much energy a Pure human soul holds. It's unimaginable, and it can be harnessed for either good or evil. Whichever side controls the soul would tip the balance."

"But if that's the case, why didn't Chase try to take me?"

"The energy in a Pure can, under normal circumstances, be claimed after death. If an otherworldly being, say a demon, should spot the soul as it ascends to heaven, it is able to take that soul. To claim it. Unfortunately we've meddled in fate. I believe, as I'm sure others will, that because the energy within you is now active, that you will have to willingly agree to hand it over." Heckle frowned. "I'm sure Chase knows you would never willingly allow him to gain the power to destroy his brother. My guess is that he believes you won't be able to take down Malphi, which will enable him to bargain for removal of the cuff."

Just like my brother to assume victory before the battle even began. My gaze fell to Sam's wrist. The cuff looked slightly different than it had before. It was tighter, and the color darker. The symbols were lighter. "What will that thing do to her?"

Heckle's expression was grim. "All demon cuffs are different. This particular one will siphon her life force until there's nothing left—and in Sam's case, it will work quickly. My best guess is that unless you can find a way to break that link between the two of you, the cuff will kill you in a matter of days. If you could break the link—"

"The link?" I started for him, but Sam beat me to it. "What the hell does that have to do with anything?"

Heckle didn't struggle. "Why do you think I told you to calm down? The higher your emotions get, the faster the siphon works."

"And that has *what* to do with the link?"

"You're tied to a demon, Sam," Heckle said with a roll of his eyes. He gently pushed her away as a car passed by, the driver leaning on his horn. "And not just any demon, but a Tainted. A Son of Cain. That comes with some hefty drawbacks."

"Drawbacks?" I was instantly alert. If he knew that the link was dangerous, why the hell was he just saying something now? "What kind of drawbacks are we talking here?"

"As far as demon infested humans go, you're not a bad guy, but at the end of the day, you're still you. And *you* have some significant darkness. She can feel your emotions through the link whether she realizes it or not. Since the cuff heightens her emotional state, the stronger the intensity, the faster the decline. It's like you're polluting her."

"*Polluting* her?"

"Stand too close to a fire and you'll get burned. Rub up against a muddy car and you'll get dirty. It's inevitable." Heckle frowned. "You're rubbing off on her, Jax. Literally. She's feeding on your emotions through the link, which in turn, is amplifying the speed at which the cuff works. You need to keep a level head, or you're going to drive her right into the grave."

Was he fucking serious? "I have a demon buried inside me. How the hell do you suggest I keep a *level head*?" I yelled over the passing traffic.

In response, Sam cursed behind me and the scent of anger in the air intensified. Shit. In the back of my mind, a voice whispered, "I told you so," over and over. I was essentially poisoning the person she was. This was why I'd left Harlow to begin with—to avoid destroying her by simply being myself.

"As for what you were doing when I arrived…" Heckle held up his hand. "Obviously the deal you made can't squelch your feelings for each other. A little tongue action here and there isn't going to bring the world crashing down. But that's as far as it can go for now."

"We haven't—" Except we had. We'd been toeing the line for weeks now, taking things farther and farther, unconcerned by the possible ramifications.

"I'm serious." His lips pressed into a hard line. "It must not go too far. The consequences would be far more damaging than you can imagine."

"What does that mean? If I kiss her my dick falls off?"

"That would be a bit dramatic." He laughed. "And as I said, a little smooch here and there won't end the world, but don't go farther than that."

Sam's eyes grew wide. "Wait. 'Don't go farther than that,' meaning we *could*?"

Heckle frowned. "You have free will, Sam. There's nothing physically standing in your way... But I advise you not to test the deal's limits. You especially won't like the result."

I opened my mouth to protest, but Heckle kept going.

"Your jobs—my job—is about maintaining balance. Keeping things even. Every happiness must be balanced out by suffering. Each failure must be countered by a win. It is the only way to keep the world spinning." He fixed his gaze on me, expression grim. "Being kept away from Sam, from having her in your life the way you want, makes you suffer. Your suffering maintains the balance of something else. It's a never ending string of events. In order for you to get what you want, someone else must lose."

"Right now I don't give a shit about balance. We need that cuff off her. If killing this demon is the way to do it, then I'm for it."

But apparently Azi wasn't.

A series of flashes, frenzied and intense, nearly brought me to my knees. I stumbled back, hands reaching for the car to steady myself as I forced the air back into my lungs.

"Jax?" Sam's voice was a beacon, pulling me from the fog.

Heckle came to stand in front of me. His somber expression, the way his brows knitted together to form a deep V, made me edgy. "I take it Azirak isn't happy about the target?"

There was only one reason Azirak wouldn't be happy about the target. "Malphi is from Azi's faction, isn't it?"

"I'm afraid so. The demon you're after is Azirak's second in command." Heckle paused. "Its...intended."

Sam frowned. "Intended what?"

"Fuck." The walls felt like they were closing in. Another series of flashes, this time involving the dark female figure I'd seen back at the house. My skin prickled, nerve endings igniting like the sun. The breath shot from my lungs. "Malphi is Azirak's mate, isn't it?"

Heckle only shrugged. "I told you there were complications…"

Chapter Eight

"What about the cuff?" I sucked in a breath, refusing to meet Jax's stare. He hadn't taken his eyes off me, and despite the buzzy feeling of anger still simmering beneath the surface, I wanted to reach out and touch him. If I could just feel his skin beneath my fingers, everything would be all right. "You don't think Azi will let us kill Malphi?"

Heckle frowned. "To be honest, I'm not sure."

"That's not helpful," I ground out, taking another deep breath. The urge to lunge forward and shake Heckle until he gave us something useful was almost overwhelming. Was this how Jax felt all the time, walking around with a storm brewing just beneath the surface? How the hell did he do it?

Jax clenched his fists. "We need to find Malphi and get Chase to remove the cuff. If that means beheading the demon, then so be it. Do you have any suggestions on where we should start?"

"That's easier said than done, I'm afraid. Demon pairings

are strong. It's ingrained in their nature. Even ones that
haven't been consummated yet. I have doubts that Azirak will
allow you to kill Malphi—and I am betting Chase knows that.
This is a win for him either way. If you fail, he can use the cuff
to bargain for Sam's power. If you succeed, then he doesn't
have Malphi to deal with."

I shifted, pulling the sleeves of my shirt down over my
fingertips. There was a sudden chill in the air. "Why is he so
worried about Malphi?"

"She is the mate of his sworn enemy. A motivated one,
at that. Jax has already refused to kill Chase once. Malphi
will not suffer the same attack of conscience. As long as Jax
remains in control of Azi, its mate is the greatest threat to
Zenak."

I didn't like the expression on Jax's face. His eyes had
glassed over, lips hitched up just a hair. I'd seen it a hundred
times, each time the demon communicated with him. After a
moment he blinked, jaw clenched tight. "We need to get the
cuff off on our own."

"Azi?" I tried to keep the fear from my voice, but I failed.
Whatever it was that the demon had shown him, it'd shaken
Jax.

"I'm worried Heckle is right," he snarled. There was
frustration in his eyes, but also the smallest hint of doubt. Of
defeat. If Azi truly wanted to prevent us from harming its
mate, we'd have a fight on our hands. And if it came down
to either me or Malphi, I didn't think I could say with one
hundred percent certainty that I would win. "It—we need
another option."

"I can offer one possibility, but the chance is slim," Heckle
said. "There's a man in the Hunter's Trail Mountains, at the
top of the highest peak. He might be able to help you."

"Why?" Jax asked. "Who is he?"

"The Archangel Michael."

"The Archangel Michael lives on top of Hunter's Trail?"

I didn't want to feel hope. Hope was dangerous. It could lift you high then send you plummeting at breakneck speed. Hope could shatter you beyond recovery. Still, I couldn't help it. A small bit seeped in. Or, maybe it came from Jax. I couldn't tell anymore what was mine and what was his.

"He can get the cuff off?" Jax asked, coming to stand beside me. It took all my reserve not to slip my hand into his. "I thought only Chase—or his death—could remove it."

Heckle stepped away from the car and brushed both hands down the front of his jacket, a completely human gesture. "I truly don't know. This situation is fairly complex, as Pures are extremely rare. An activated Pure walking the earth is unprecedented. One linked to a demon royal… We're swimming in uncharted waters here. We don't know how the cuff will react. Chase has the upper hand here, I'm afraid. If Michael has no solution to offer, then you won't have a choice if you want to save Sam. You will have to kill Malphi and hope Chase keeps his word."

"*I'm* not a royal of hell," Jax snarled. A rush of anger rippled through him, and by default, into me. "And if it comes down to it, I *will* kill Malphi. No one, no *thing*, will stop me." I had a feeling Jax was talking more to Azi than to us.

Heckle frowned, then glared like he could see through my skull. "I know Azirak cares for Sam, but do not underestimate the ties it has to Malphi." He didn't have to worry about that. The demon and I had shared a few *moments*, but I had no delusions that the demon would choose me over its mate. It sounded risky, but going to Michael seemed like a more solid bet.

"We'll go see Michael. Hunter's Trail is six hours from here. That would still leave us with a full day. But if he can't help us…" I shuddered. "How do we find Malphi?" The thought of cutting down random demons until we found the one we were looking for was oddly—not to mention disturbingly— comforting, but we didn't have time.

Heckle shrugged. "No clue. That's your job—but something tells me you won't have to look hard. It's going to want to get its claws in both of you as soon as possible. If you're going to try Michael, make it to him before they find you. But be warned, if he can give you help, it will not come free."

"So he'll want, what? Like, payment?" Something told me the archangel Michael didn't take credit cards.

"Yes," Heckle said. "For Michael to grant you this favor, you will need to give something in return. Something to level the playing field."

"To provide balance," I finished. Jax was right. This balance crap was getting old.

"Why?" Jax barked. Fists balled tight, he slammed a hand against the roof of the car. "Why should she have to pay anything? This isn't her fault. It's not even mine. It's yours. You threw us into this without warning. If you hadn't killed her and brought her back, we wouldn't be in this mess. They wouldn't know who she was."

Heckle's expression darkened. For the first time, I saw real fury in his eyes. "I would advise you to watch your tone." He took a deep breath and some of the tension left him. "And while that may be partially true, the situation with Malphi would have arisen regardless. Chase will always be looking for a way to get to you. Since demons recycle and are reborn into human bodies again and again, Malphi would be searching for you regardless. You were never free, Jax. Never safe. So long as a demon resides inside you, you never will be."

"What kind of balance," I asked, stepping between them. A fight between heaven's original Balance Agent, and a demon royal was the last thing my frayed nerves needed. "I don't have anything to give."

Heckle held my gaze for a moment. There was a spark of regret, but it was there and gone almost too quickly to notice. "There is always something left to give, Sam."

"This is such bullshit," I spat, and while a part of me was horrified, another part felt exhilarated. The anger felt good. Like a warm blanket on a cold winter's night.

Jax pushed harder on the gas pedal, and the speedometer passed sixty-five. We were well into Burke now, the map he'd picked up at the gas station wedged in the console between us.

"Sammy, please calm down. For one thing, getting pissed isn't going to help the situation. And aside from that, I hate being the calm one. The voice of reason sounds fucked up coming from me. Okay?" He looked like he expected me to go nuclear or something. "How about something to eat?" he asked, veering toward the ramp to exit the highway. There was a row of choices on the main road. All fast food. All greasy and disgusting. All sounding good.

"I'm starving," I admitted. I couldn't remember the last time I'd eaten. It had to be yesterday, before work. Yesterday, when my world was less complicated. Or at least, slightly less. Ever since Jax walked back into my life, things had been a little rocky.

He nodded and pulled the car into the parking lot of a small deli. It was old, with peeling paint and huge potholes in the lot, but I didn't care. I would have agreed to eat sushi if that was all there was—and I hated sushi. "Stay here. I'll grab something and be right back."

I waited until he was out of sight before pushing open the door and sliding out to stretch my legs. Everything had started to cramp from sitting still for so long. I'd never been good at extended car rides, and it probably didn't help that I was wound tighter than fishing line.

Was this what my life would be like from now on? Dodging the greedy, grabby hands of heaven and hell? All because I was the unlucky recipient of *Pure* genes? I might not have it all figured out yet—as Aunt Kelly pointed out on a daily basis—but I knew damn well what I *didn't* want. And that was to live my life running away.

"Excuse me." A woman approached the car with a tentative smile. She came from the store next to the deli, a plastic bag in her hands. "Any idea what time it is?"

I pulled the cell from my pocket. "Just after one."

"Damn it," the woman muttered. "Late as usual." She looked to the road. "Any chance you know a shortcut to Parker Avenue?"

"Sorry. Not really from around here." I followed her gaze to my wrist, to the demon cuff. Every hair on my body jumped to attention. Oh, seriously? Some random person approaches and asks the time? *The time*? Really?

She came a little closer, squinting. "Wow. That's an interesting bracelet."

I reached behind me, feeling for the door handle. When I found it, I slipped my fingers beneath the latch and yanked upward, but it didn't budge. Locked. Awesome. Mistake number two. I was batting a thousand today.

The woman shot me a deceptively warm smile.

"This thing?" I asked. "Junk jewelry. See that huge guy inside the deli? My boyfriend. He got it out of one of those vending machines. Kind of a joke."

The woman set the plastic bag down on the blacktop by her feet and smiled. This time, it was predatory. Hungry and…wrong. She closed her eyes and gave a dramatic roll of her head. When she opened them, her dark brown eyes had turned blazing orange. "I know who he is." Another step.

"And I know what you are. You're a wonderment."

Without Jax, I had no chance of fending off a demon—or whatever the hell this thing was—on my own. Unless I had a secret set of super powers—and I hadn't seen any sign of them—I was in trouble. My only chance was to run. A head to head fight and I was going to get squashed like a bug.

I sighed and bent my head, making like I was about to surrender. Instead though, I stepped forward and brought my left elbow up, hard, like I'd seen Jax do. It connected with her jaw, and I cringed as pins and needles exploded beneath my skin and rocketed down my arm. She stumbled away, distracted, and I dashed off in the opposite direction. I got to the edge of the building, and just around the corner, before I ran into her again.

Literally.

Impossibly.

I backed up, staring into greedy eyes as she smiled. "Silly human. Outrunning us is impossible. Our minions are everywhere."

"Sounds exhausting," I said, taking another step back. My heart hammered an erratic rhythm inside my chest.

"Come with me and you won't be harmed."

"I don't know you well enough to go home with you. Plus, you're not really my type." I swallowed and continued my slow retreat.

"We feared you would be difficult," she said, utterly calm. It was her unruffled demeanor, more than the menacing tone, that rattled me. Like she was positive this would go her way. And why wouldn't she be? I was, after all, only human.

I shrugged and kept inching backward. With a nervous laugh, I said, "Yeah? Well, making it easy on demons isn't really my style."

"*Demon*?" The woman laughed, a trilling echo that hurt my ears. "I'm no such filthy thing!"

A rush of air blew into my face and something large—no, huge—fluttered open and loomed above my head. "Wings," I breathed. A massive expanse of jet black feathers filled the small space. "You're—"

"An angel." She tilted her head to the left, then to the right, studying me as though I was something alien. "And you are human. I do not understand why you align yourself with darkness. We are forces of good. We wish to eradicate the demons. To free the world."

"That sounds noble and all, but Heckle said—"

The angel hissed and spat. "Heckle." She said the name as if it were the vilest of curses. "He is nothing more than God's pitiful attempt at clinging to something that was lost long ago. He felt it was his fault that Cain killed Abel. His design, flawed. But the world is meant to be flawed." She stepped closer, fists clutched tight. The movement was aggressive. Menacing. "It is meant to be violent."

I backed away. "That's kind of a contradiction. A minute ago, you said you wanted to get rid of the demons. Now all of a sudden you've got a lust for violence? Someone needs to go back on their meds…"

"If there is no violence, then we have no place here. No purpose." Her eyes blazed from black to fiery orange. "*We* are needed to maintain balance, not Heckle. It was our job. Then more and more Tainted walked the earth. He became more important. We, less so. Now he controls the power. He holds our fate in his hands. God's favorite." She spat again. "A wretched little cur."

"Tell me how you really feel." I inched another step into the alley.

"We were content to obey. That is our lot. But then you came. Your kind rarely survives to adulthood, yet *you* did. Somehow you've been activated and now, who pulls your strings and controls your power? The Master of Balance."

"No one pulls my strings or controls me," I said as calmly as possible. "And I'm just a girl. Nothing special."

She laughed. A broken, distorted sound that was nothing close to being human. "A mortal, yes. But nothing special? Either you take me for a fool, or you are ignorant." Another step closer. "Either way, you belong to us. You are Pure."

"Pure?" Maybe if I played dumb, she'd let her guard down. Give me an advantage. "Honey, that ship sailed a long time ago."

She shot forward, closing the distance between us, and screamed, a horrific sound that made the very air blur and brought me to my knees. Arms much stronger than they appeared wrapped around my waist, roughly hauling me to my feet as a rush of wind blew over me. What little sun shone into the alley was blotted out and the air seemed to thin. Breathing was harder, if not nearly impossible, and something soft and feathery brushed the side of my face.

But just as suddenly as it all began, it ended. The air rushed back, along with the light, and the angel fell away. Eyes wide, she collapsed to the ground, leaving a tall, dark figure with black-rimmed eyes towering behind. In his hands was the thing's heart.

Jax dropped the gore-coated mass and stepped over the dead angel. He stalked forward and grabbed my face, yanking it to his. Our lips met, fierce and desperate, as the tips of his fingers curled around small sections of my hair. He pulled on my bottom lip, tongue skating across then slipping inside. For a blissful moment, the kiss made me forget about the hell hanging over our heads.

When he finally pulled away, I watched his eyes change. They went from solid black, to thinly lined, to their normal, beautiful gray. "Did it hurt you?"

I shook my head. "No. But it did escalate things."

He looked from me to the angel. "How so?"

I stared at him. Was he kidding? "Do you not see what this thing is?"

He blinked and nudged the angel with the toe of his boot, glancing from me to the corpse again. A single black feather fluttered free and landed at his feet. "...dead?"

I double checked, just to make sure I hadn't lost my mind. Nope. They were still there. Two huge black feather-covered appendages protruding from either side of her back. "Wings?" I said. "An angel?"

He laughed. "Sammy, come on—"

"Jax," I snapped. I had no clue why he couldn't see the wings, but they were there. I bent to retrieve the feather and held it out for him to see. "Where do you think this came from?"

He blinked several times, squinting. "Sammy, there's nothing in your hand." Palm resting flat against my forehead, he cocked a brow and said, "You sure you're okay?"

"Fine then." I dropped the feather. "You can't see it for whatever reason, but that woman *was* an angel."

"An *angel* attacked you? Doesn't that go against the whole good versus evil thing?"

Was attacked the right word? She hadn't hurt me, though I was fairly sure she would have if that what it would have taken to snap me up. "Heckle said both sides will stop at nothing to keep the other from getting their hands on me. That means we have heaven, hell, your demon-infused brother, *and* Azi's demonic-woman-scorned on our asses. Did anyone ever tell you that you come with a shit load of baggage?"

His lip twitched. "Tired of me already?" At the other end of the alley, something clattered. Jax cursed. "We need to go."

Chapter Nine

JAX

Five minutes. I'd been gone five fucking minutes. If I hadn't returned when I did—shit. No reason to go there. She was safe. Other than being shaken, Sam was fine. And the whole *angel* thing? Yeah. I had no fucking clue what to think about that. "You doing okay?"

The murky swirl of emotion surrounding her filled the car, infused with the distinct hint of gray, making it hard for me to concentrate on the road. Azi nibbled at it, taking small bites, but all it did was make the thing more unsettled. It was hungry and we were approaching the danger line. I'd need to feed it something more substantial soon or control was going to become an issue.

"I'm good," she said quietly.

"Are you?" The hazy mist surged. It coiled around her like tiny snakes, tendrils circling chunks of her hair and neck, with stragglers entwining her arms. I'd never seen emotion so thick. "Because you don't seem okay."

She stared down at her hand, running her thumb along the black metal band. "I'm just a little thrown by all this."

"Thrown?" If things weren't headed up Shit Creek I might have smiled at the understatement.

"A few months ago everything was normal. I was a normal girl—damaged, but normal—trying to make it in the world. School, minimum wage jobs, a pile of bills… It all comes back to that damn party. The one at Huntington where I was attacked. Everything changed that night, even if I didn't know it at the time. If I'd never gone—"

"I used to think like that. *What if.* What if I'd had the balls to off myself instead of leaving home? What if I'd stayed away instead of keeping tabs on you, watching from the shadows? Would Chase have even targeted you? What if I'd never left to begin with… Would things have turned out differently if I'd just come clean?" The gray smoke started to ribbon with blue. "The answer is, who gives a shit?"

She turned toward me, mouth agape.

"Seriously, Sammy. Why ask questions that are irrelevant? We can't go back. We can only go forward. The past can't be changed, but the future can be adapted to. And we will," I said with ferocity. "We *will* adapt. It's who we are, you and me. Fighters. Always have been. Always will be."

She sighed and looked up. It was hard to keep my eyes on the road and my hands on the wheel, knowing she was so conflicted. "Maybe it's the cuff," she said. "It all feels so hopeless."

"I know it feels that way, but it's not. We've been through a lot together. We'll get through this, too."

She didn't answer, but the gray waves of fear, swirling and reaching for everything, seemed to diminish just a little. A moment later, her hand, so small and soft, slipped beneath mine on the console between us.

I drove until just after midnight before pulling off the highway and into the parking lot of the first motel I found. The Star Rise Inn was a dive, but it was cheap and out of the way. I should have gotten us two rooms, but letting Sam out of my sight was a bad idea. Plus, we didn't have the cash. The Viking paid out once every two weeks, and I was new to the whole budgeting thing.

"You want the shower first?" she asked, sitting on the bed to pull off her sneakers. She faced me, and as she bent down, the neckline of her T-shirt fell forward to reveal…

Shit.

I picked my eyes, and my jaw, off the floor and cleared my throat. "Nah. You go first. I'll check to make sure everything is sealed tight and secure."

When I looked again, she was grinning. She shrugged and stood, turning slowly to face the wall. "Have it your way."

I waited for her to head into the bathroom, but she stayed where she was, back to me and head bent low. A moment later, she peeked over her shoulder, through a curtain of satiny hair, and undid the buttons of her jeans. Slowly, deliberately, she inched them down. Over her hips. Down her thighs. When she couldn't reach any more, she bent at the waist, much farther than she needed to, and proceeded to slide the denim to her ankles.

An image of me rushing forward and grabbing her from behind rampaged through my mind. Right hand twisted around chunks of her long brown hair, I pulled back hard, tilting her head as far as it would go. My left hand kneaded her breast, sliding down to the waistband of her underwear. A moment of hesitation and then they slipped inside, fingers plunging into warm, heavenly folds.

She pushed back against me, the most delectable moan

coming from deep in her throat as I moved my fingers in a circular motion. Her breath quickened, and—

The vision faded to black. In a way, the abrupt ending was worse than seeing it through. It left me raw and wanting, a single, twitching nerve in need of attention. "Sammy, don't…"

"What?" She tossed her hair and peered over her shoulder again. Her grin was wicked. She knew exactly what she did to me. The way she twisted things up and set fire to my veins. "You can't touch, but no one said you couldn't look." She stepped out of the jeans and faced me again, hooking both her thumbs into the waist of her barely-there thong. "You *do* want to look, right? I can feel it."

Reason said turn around and walk out the door. Wait for things to cool off. She was jacked up on my emotions and desires, picking them up through the damn link. That's the only reason she'd do this—purposefully try to drive me insane. It made spending any amount of time together as dangerous as a carload of Molotov Cocktails. There wasn't any second of the day I didn't think about her. No moment passed without fantasizing what it would be like to touch her. If it was true, and the link between us dumped even a fraction of my emotion into her, then we were a nuclear warhead waiting for detonation.

Because the cold, hard truth was there really was no such thing as *just looking* when it came to her. I still felt the vision. The length of her pressed up against me. The sounds she made. The feel of her on my fingertips, warm and slick. I was suffocating and Sam was the air.

I was on the other side of my bed, close to the door. Two steps. Maybe three. I could be out in the cool air in less than ten seconds.

Or I could be on the other side of the room in three.

I sailed over the bed. She fell forward onto her own mattress, and I was on her. "I need so much more than a look," I whispered. As in the vision, I grabbed a handful of her long hair and pulled back so that I could whisper in her ear. "There is no way for me to simply look at you without touching. I want you. *It* wants you. Do you have any fucking idea what that feels like?"

She shimmied, twisting her body to create a friction that made my eyes roll back. "I know what it feels like," she said, her voice almost a growl. "And I know it's against the rules, but I don't care."

I let go of her hair and shifted my weight, then turned her so that we were eye to eye. Her colors swirled, a mix of orange and pink—lust and hope—blazing against the muddiness. The demon stirred, its desire to feed overridden only by the craving it had for Sam. It was a war. Between my body and my mind. Between my word and my need. The demon's need. Sam was a magnet and the pull was uncompromising. Relentless. I was nothing more than an object caught in her orbit.

I kissed her. Fierce. Savage. Our lips moved together, rough and bruising, and she was all there was. The demon inside shuddered with a wave of contentment at having gotten its way. *Our way*. But beneath that was the sting. The building pain that came from my happiness. It wasn't something I could prevent—demons couldn't stomach human happiness—and in that moment neither Azi nor I cared. All that mattered was the sensation of Sam beneath my fingers.

She moaned into my mouth and pushed up against me. The thin layers of fabric that separated us were too restricting. I needed to feel her. All of her. I grabbed the edge of my shirt and tugged it over my head, then yanked hers up. It snagged just below her chin. Sam reached for it, but as far as I was concerned, it was wasted time. I seized her wrists, dragging them above her head and pinning them there.

"If we—what will happen if—"

I reclaimed her lips, savoring the faint taste of cherries

that lingered from her Chap Stick. The kiss left no room for argument. No allowance for questions. We were past that now. A boulder rolling downhill.

"I don't give a fuck," I whispered, pulling away just enough to speak. I reached for the button of my jeans and yanked down the zipper. As soon as I did, everything went to hell.

The keening sound was like a bomb going off inside my head, but it stirred a feeling deep inside. A primal instinct that drowned out all good sense. The flash came next—a darkened female form writhing beneath me. It whispered strange words I didn't understand, yet the sound of them ignited something feral and raw. Azi surged beneath my skin, pushing for dominance. Demanding it. I gave in, unable to pull myself from the intensity of Sam's touch, and surrendered wholly to the demon. My movements became its own. My hands, Azirak's tools. It hooked my fingers around the waistband of Sam's underwear and tugged an inch. Then, another. She faded in and out, oscillating between herself and the faceless female demon.

Malphi. The female was Malphi.

Knowing this, I should have pulled away, but the need grew stronger. Undeniable.

Azirak lowered my lips to Sam's stomach, planting a trail of hungry kisses southward. She gasped and arched off the bed. The sound was like fire, consuming everything and mingling with the darkest parts of me, the parts that lay hidden in the deepest corners of my soul.

The parts that belonged to the demon.

My vision swam. The impassioned sounds she made were carnal in the rawest sense—and wrong. One moment it was Sam, the next, Malphi. Azirak reveled in it, the semblance of complete freedom overtaking me. I'd never felt anything like it. Powerful and limitless, in that moment I could do anything without consequence. Control the world and take the things I desired. And there was only one thing I wanted.

Sam...

Malphi.

Sammy...

Malphi.

The need grew until it exploded, like a bomb going off in a confined space. It jolted me, and I knew this was wrong. Dangerous in so many ways. I struggled for control, and Azi fought like it never had before.

Strange words echoed inside my head, threatening to break my skull in half. I didn't understand them, but Azirak did.

We can be whole again... Feast on the human as my essence looms, lay claim to her power then come to me, my lord...

I jerked away, stumbling over the edge of the bed and falling back against my own. My heart pounded, a thunderous beat drowning out everything else in the room. The thoughts in my mind tore me apart, then put me back together only to do it again. The darkness. The violence. The willingness to submit...

Sam knelt in front of me, taking my face in her hands. Her lips moved, but I couldn't hear her voice. I gripped the edge of the bed until my fingers went numb. Azi had settled, but I still felt it—how it had wanted to do as Malphi asked, was overcome by the need to possess.

"Jax, please. Tell me what happened."

"Pain," I lied. "I guess that's why Heckle told us not to test the limits."

"Jesus." Her expression was all concern, and I felt guilty for lying.

I climbed to my feet as she did the same. "It was like someone set off an atomic bomb inside my head."

"Sounds painful."

"I don't recommend it," I responded, keeping my eyes down. The T-shirt she had on came just below her waist, leaving a thin scrap of lacy black peeking out. One look and I was in an entirely new world of hell. If we started again, I knew there'd be no stopping it.

"Why didn't it happen right away, though?" I heard her sigh. "We, um, got kind of far…"

"I guess there's a limit." I turned away, unable to look her in the eyes. "Heckle said a kiss wouldn't do it, but much more than that would cross the line. I guess we found our trigger."

Sam was in front of me, tipping my face up to meet hers. She opened her mouth, then closed it again, shaking her head slowly. "He's right, Jax. I mean, obviously I want to be with you on my own, but Heckle is right. I can feel how much you want me, and it's making me careless. Right now, I can feel the urge you have to—"

A million X-rated images unfolded before my eyes. "Do not finish that sentence, Sammy. *Please*."

"You've never been good with impulse control," she said, voice dropping. "And if I really was riding your…bad vibes…I might suggest that, since we now know our limit, we should—"

I covered her mouth with my hand. If she kept going, I would cave. If I caved, who knew what would happen? "Go. Take a shower."

"Are you sure?" She tugged at the collar of her shirt. "I could—"

I gripped the edge of the bed harder and squeezed my eyes closed. "Please, Sammy. Get the hell away from me."

Chapter Ten

SAM

The water had been hot and the pressure just right. Still, it hadn't alleviated the tension in my muscles. I'd been standing right next to Jax when Heckle gave his warning. We didn't know if it pertained to me or him, but it'd been clear. Break the rules and pay the price. We both knew…and neither one of us had cared. Even now, after knowing it had hurt him, I wanted to slide from the bed and make him kiss me again.

That was the drawback to Jax and me. It'd been that way for as far back as I could remember. We ignored everything and lived to keep each other sane and safe. Then when things between us changed, nothing else mattered. It was all about us. Screw the world.

I rolled over and pulled the covers with me, burrowing deep. They smelled of cigarettes and stale beer, but I didn't care. I was too tired, both mentally and physically exhausted. Thoughts of Jax, of the pain he was in, and the danger that hung over our heads, played on repeat inside my head. The lingering memory of what we'd almost done, coupled with the fact that he was laying a few feet away, made my pulse quicken and my skin warm.

The cuff was heavy and growing tighter with each moment that passed. When I'd slid into bed, it was just past three in the morning. I'd been wearing this thing for almost twenty-four hours now. One day down. Only two left.

I looked down at the cuff and it contracted as if responding to my scrutiny. I'd actually forgotten about it for a while. Jax had that effect on me. Even when we were kids, he had a way of making my problems and fears fade until they were nothing more than harmless shadows on the wall. I wanted to be that for him, too. To be the thing that grounded him. But instead I'd instigated an act that had caused him pain. The skin beneath the black metal band twitched and I fought a shiver. An act that, despite what had happened as a result, I wanted to instigate again.

I shifted, this time rolling onto my back. The clock cast a faint glow on the ceiling. It was reflected on the television, the light playing off the bare bulb in the ceiling overhead. But there was something else. A faint rustling sound coming from just beyond the door.

I threw off the covers and, sliding out of bed as quietly as possible, crept across the carpet and put my ear to the door. The sound was almost like an animal scratching against the wood.

"What the hell?" Jax groaned from underneath the covers. The light beside his bed flickered to life. He shifted around, peering at me through the dim light with groggy annoyance.

"I dunno," I said, pushing away from the door. "I thought I heard something."

He shoved off the covers with a grunt and swung his legs over the edge of the bed. The floorboards groaned as he padded barefoot across the room and stopped beside me. "Like what?"

I put my ear to the door again. Everything was quiet. Maybe I was losing my mind. "Nothing. I was probably dreaming."

Without a word, he started back across the room. But he only got halfway to the bed when a knock stopped him. Quirking a brow, he turned and tilted his head. "Expecting someone?"

"Yeah." I dove for my jeans and tugged them on. "I ordered a stripper."

With a roll of his eyes and a finger to his lips, he backed toward the door. There was no peep hole, so he moved the curtains aside a fraction of an inch. "Looks human," he said with a snort. "Then again, who the hell knows?"

"So, harmless?"

He turned to me, a spark of mischief in his eyes. A rush of warmth rippled through me. "You're human and you're far from harmless."

I flipped him off and nodded to the door. "Safe to answer—"

The guy on the other side of the door began to pound.

I crept a little closer. The door rattled and shook. "Someone wants in real bad."

Jax moved between me and the door, holding his hand high in an attempt keep me back. "What the hell does he want? It's after three a.m."

"Open the door and find out. He's human, right? The manager maybe? What could he possibly do?"

The man decided to answer my question personally. The door blew open in a hail of wooden splinters and the guy walked in, eyes glowing a fiery orange and an axe in his hand.

Jax looked from him to me and shrugged. "Depends on how you feel about the axe."

Our new guest let out a hair-curling sound—a cross between a howl and a yell—and swung his weapon. The blade imbedded itself in the dresser by the door. It was deep, wedged solidly in the wood. There should have been no way for him to pull it free so easily. But he did. Like pulling a loose thread on the end of a shirt, he lifted the axe from the wood and swung it again. This time, it passed so close to Jax that his hair fluttered.

He jumped back, hand up to block the next attack.

"What's wrong with his eyes?" I screamed, stumbling back as Jax nearly knocked me over in his attempt to avoid the blade.

"Wicked contacts?" he called, dodging another blow. The man roared and dropped the axe, launching himself forward. He collided with Jax, sending them both clear across the room. He hammered a series of blows to his head, followed by another to the throat—Jax sputtered and coughed, gasping for air.

If he was human, the guy had been sucking down otherworldly steroids. Except… I thought back to the angel in the alley, to the way her eyes blazed like fire. "Jax!" I made my way around the room, trying to steer clear of the chaos. "Don't hurt him."

"Don't hurt—" The man hit him again, knocking Jax to the ground. "Are you insane?" he yelled. "He just swung an axe at me!"

Our minions are everywhere.

"His eyes," I called as the man whirled on me. His blank expression was as disturbing as any demonic scowl I'd ever come face-to-face with. "The color. Something the angel in the alley said. I think the angel is controlling him."

"The *angel* is dead," Jax yelled. He swung at the man, and I couldn't help gasping when his hand came up, catching Jax's fist like he was swatting a fly. Before I could blink, he lashed out with his other hand, the blow connecting with the side of Jax's head. He went down hard.

"You must come with me." His voice rang with an eerie echo. He whirled away from Jax and grabbed my arm. I tried to pull away, but his grip was like iron—and just as cold.

He turned and started toward the door, dragging me along. I glanced over my shoulder. Jax was on the floor where he'd fallen. He wasn't moving. The air turned frigid. He was okay. Just knocked out. I'd know if it was more than that. We were linked, right?

Out the door and into the darkness—the guy didn't stop. I fought, but it was as pointless as trying to light a match in a tornado. We passed rows of doors, all silent and dark, and waltzed right past the manager's desk. "Hey," I screamed. "Do something. This guy won't let go of me!"

The guy behind the counter, a tall, thin man with horn rim glasses and a roman nose, came bounding out the door. He looked from the man to me, brows furrowed. "Everything okay here?"

"No," I screamed. Did anything about this situation look normal? "Not okay. Help me out here!"

It wasn't fair to involve him. He was human and had no idea what he was up against, but my terror made me selfish. I was apparently the Holy Grail for both heaven and hell. I had no idea what they would do once they got their hands on me, and I had no desire to find out.

The motel employee grabbed the guy's arm and tugged back. "I don't think the lady wants to go with you, man."

With a single shove from the fiery-eyed man, the Good Samaritan flew across the parking lot. But when my abductor tried to move forward, he ran into a small roadblock. Well, not really so small. Jax was there, cloaked in shadow and larger than life. He stepped forward, a single move that shifted him into the beam of light coming from the streetlamp a few feet away. If I didn't know him—if I had no idea what a good man he was—I would have been terrified by the deranged look in his eyes.

They were black. Not rimmed in inky darkness like they had been recently, but solid and bottomless. Usually that meant Azi had taken control. *Usually*. This time, it was all Jax, I was sure. The actions were different, the way he held himself and the way he moved. I saw the rise and fall of his shoulders as he breathed, and the subtly twitching muscle in his neck. When the demon seized control, it was eerily still.

"Mind jacked or not, if you don't let her go now, I *will* kill you." His voice was low and dangerous. He leaned forward a bit, and the grin that split his lips made me shudder with trepidation. "And I promise you, I *will* love it."

"You cannot kill this human," the man said. His grip on my arm tightened. "He is an innocent."

Jax laughed. "Someone's been feeding you bad info. I can, and will." He came a step closer. "And innocent? I don't think so. He's latched on to my girl. That's as far from innocent as you can get in my eyes."

"Do not pretend you want this human for anything other than to use her, demon."

Another step. "Power means shit to me. *She's* important to me. The most important."

"Hell will not gain her power."

"No, it won't. Because hell ain't getting its hands on her." Jax shot forward. "And neither are you."

The man didn't flinch. Pivoting, he avoided Jax and spun me out of reach. I tripped, going down hard on my knees. "You cannot fight us," the man said with complete calm. It was creepy. His expression never changed, and his movements, so controlled, were like the precise mechanics of a machine.

Jax roared and made another swipe. This time he caught the man's head between his hands and, without hesitation, twisted. It happened so fast yet at the same time was so incredibly detailed. The man's neck rotated at a wholly unnatural angle and the orange light in his eyes flickered then died, leaving behind a dull, lifeless brown. His grip on my arm fell away and his hand went slack just before his body crumpled to the concrete. It was soundless, like something from a dream, or a scene on the television with the volume turned off. It stayed like that. Eerily quiet, just Jax and me standing there staring down at the dead man—until a shrill scream shattered the silence.

On the sidewalk, a woman with a small suitcase stood, her mouth open in horror.

"Let's go," Jax said, grabbing my arm and dragging me away. All our stuff was still in the room, but there was no time to go back. Jax had the keys, and we were in the car in moments and peeling from the parking lot.

Chapter Eleven

The sun was up before we stopped again. The car needed gas, and thankfully Sam had kept her credit card and license in her jeans' pocket. The motel was a close call. I wouldn't make that mistake again. I didn't care if I had to keep her locked in the car from here to the mountain. No one else was taking a crack at her.

"You're quiet," she said, stretching her feet. "You need to talk to me."

I kept my eyes on the road. Chancing a look in her direction could be disastrous. Even while that man at the motel had been holding her, trying to take her away from me, my eyes caught on the curve of her neck. The way her shirt pulled taut with every breath. Her lips... I may have embraced the demon, gaining more control over its natural power, but I'd sacrificed something of myself as well. I'd fought for Sam before. Had killed without remorse. But they'd all been demons. I'd never been forced to go this far with a human.

"About?"

"You killed—"

I tightened my fingers around the wheel. "I know what I did, Sammy. And if you think I regret it, you're wrong. I did what needed to be done to keep you safe, and I would do it again in a heartbeat." And I would. Sam was the single most important thing in my life.

"Then why do you look…I dunno…upset?"

Upset was a serious misinterpretation, but I was glad. I was trying hard to keep my emotions in check. "I'm thinking," I replied. Easy. Innocent. She didn't need to know that my mind was playing out a scenario where I pulled the car to the side of the road, ripped every scrap of clothing from her body, and showed her just how much she belonged to me.

Azi rolled with it and communicated in its own desires. The pictures and feelings that came were so graphic, I flinched, and the car jerked to the right, skidding into the gravel on the side of the road before I managed to right our course.

"Jax?" came Sam's worried voice. "What's wrong?"

"Nothing." The word was sharper than I wanted, but that was fine. If she was pissed then maybe she'd stop asking questions. Questions I couldn't—and didn't want to—answer.

She sighed. "When exactly did you start lying to me?"

I ground my teeth together, clenching my jaw hard. No answer was better than biting her head off.

"Seriously, Jax. I might not be able to see your emotions, but I know how you're feeling."

"One stupid link and you think you know everything that's going on inside my head?" I yelled.

Red filled the car. "Screw the link," Sam shouted. "This is about us. The *us* that existed long before that damn thing came into play. I've known what was going on inside your thick skull since we were kids."

I pushed harder on the gas, bringing our speed to almost

eighty. "What is it you want me to say? That this sucks? That it's unfair? It is. Deal with it."

"That's what I'm trying to do," she fired back. "Deal with it. In order to deal with something, though, you have to acknowledge that there's a problem in the first place."

Sam Merrick. My reason for breathing, but also the source of every migraine I'd ever had. "Fine," I fired back, fingers digging into the wheel. "There *is* a fucking problem. I'm having a hard time controlling things."

"Things…?"

"Myself," I said with barely contained loathing.

Deep breaths. Needed to calm down. Azi was growing antsy, nipping at the tendrils of anger I put out. If I kept this up, soon it would be rabid and desperate to feed. When that happened, I would have zero control over any of my impulses. Or the demon's.

"Myself with you," I amended, keeping my eyes on the road. "Since we… Things have been harder."

"Harder, how?"

I didn't answer. What was I supposed to say? That every time I was close to her, Azi goaded me to rip her clothes off? That I didn't need the encouragement because I wanted to do that anyway? 'Cause that wouldn't make me sound like a dick? Add all that to the demon cuff, heightening and siphoning the emotions she was feeling through our link, and you had a recipe for disaster.

"I think it was easier when it was just a fantasy," Sam said quietly. "Thinking about being with you, of having you back in my life—that unattainable dream that you'd come home one day and everything would just go back to the way it was—was something that made it easier to deal with things."

"How was that easier?"

"It was easier because it was safe." She shifted in her seat so she was facing me. I didn't look at her. "At the risk of sounding corny, love is taking chances, Jax. It's misery and pain and disappointment right along with all the great stuff. You think this is easy for me? You let me down once already. You promised you'd always be there, and even though I understand why you weren't, it still stings. I think in the back of my mind, I'm waiting for you to disappear again."

I wouldn't tell her that I'd thought about it a thousand times since agreeing to Heckle's deal. The idea of walking away from her gutted me, but at the same time it felt selfish to stay. It wasn't a secret, though. She knew how I felt. Knew how, regardless of anything she said, I would always loathe myself and the things I was forced to do. Things I would always be forced to do. This was a permanent situation for me. The demon would always be riding shotgun. It would always be hungry. My life was going to be harsh and savage until the day I took my last breath. The closer I was to her, the bigger the chance of her getting caught in the crossfire when I eventually went down.

"I won't leave," I said, switching lanes. Traffic was slowing down. Roadwork, or possibly an accident, was bringing all three lanes to a standstill.

"I know," she said. "But the fear is there. It'll always be there, and that's what I mean. That's the risk."

I should have let the conversation die there, but I couldn't. "It's hard not to act on what I want when Azi wants the same thing. It…" The words caught in my throat.

"It, what?"

I made the mistake of glancing across the car. She watched me, eyes wide and lips parted slightly. "I *want* to touch you right now," I said, taking my right hand from the wheel and reaching for her leg. "Azi *needs* me to." I slipped my hand between her thighs, extending my thumb to stroke her through the denim.

"This is about the sex," she said, understanding. I couldn't read her expression, and that bothered me. Her colors were still so muddled, too many swirling together to make out any specific emotion.

"I don't know how to answer that, Sammy. Obviously, yeah, the sex is great." I chuckled. "Better than great. But for Azi it's about more than that. It's about possession. Control. It's raw and harsh and borders on uncontrollable, and what scares me is sometimes I don't care."

She snickered and placed her hand over mine, moving it to her knee. "Sounds like passion to me."

"There's something else," I admitted before I could stop myself. I took my hand back and palmed the steering wheel.

"Okay," she said carefully.

"Someone else…"

She laughed. "*Someone else?* Other than me? You know I don't buy that, right?"

Of course she didn't. Because it was as impossible as me getting through the pearly gates one day. And yet it wasn't. "I told you, I keep seeing these…scenes. Fierce, possessive scenarios that Azi keeps forcing into my head."

"You already told me this. What does it have to do—"

"Sometimes it's you. I see myself doing things…" My fingers tightened around the wheel. The leather bowed beneath my grip. "Sometimes it's someone else."

"Someone else? Like who? Another girl, you mean?" Her tone changed.

"Yes," I said. "No." Fuck. "Another female, but I don't think she's human."

"Because that makes it so much better…"

"Sammy…" I took a deep breath. "I think it's Malphi. I think—I think Azi wants its mate. The demon will try to stop me if I hunt down Malphi."

"That's not really better, either," she grumbled. "And what does that mean? For us? For me…?"

"Nothing. Nothing has changed. I said it would *try*." The words sounded convincing, but I wasn't sure I believed them. The ferocity of what I felt when Malphi appeared in my visions in human form was immeasurable. Sam was everything I wanted. Everything I'd *ever* wanted. Yet the pull toward Azirak's mate was magnetism on an entirely different level. If it came down to it, Azi would do more than try. I had a feeling it would succeed.

"If Azi wants this thing," Sam said, "then technically I'm in the way."

Azi had feelings for Sam, but it wanted its mate. I was betting Malphi felt the same. That made Sam right.

She was the only thing standing in the demoness's way...

It took the rest of the day, but still I was relieved when we finally arrived at the bottom of the mountain. By the time we reached the trailhead, the sun was about to go down. I didn't love the idea of hiking up to the top in the dark. Sitting still wasn't an option, though. The clock was ticking. We were almost at the end of day two.

We had everything working against us. Sam wouldn't say it, but the cuff was causing her pain. Every now and then, when she thought I wasn't looking, she'd wince. That, on top of being number one on heaven and hell's Most Wanted list, was making her edgy. The more we moved, the less chance that they would find her. Nightfall or not, we were heading up that mountain.

"You ready?" I asked, killing the engine. Sam's colors were a jumbled mix of confusion, fear, and sadness. I hated that she felt this way. She'd already been through so much. I hated it more because there was jack shit I could do about it.

"To drop in unannounced on the *Archangel Michael*?

Sure. Sounds like a party." She undid her seat belt and got out of the car. A wispy trail of gray followed her.

I closed the door and locked it, making my way around to where she stood looking up the hill. The trail was narrow and there was a thick chain with a sign hanging down that said that hiking was prohibited between the hours of dusk and dawn.

"Maybe this was a bad idea. If he can't help us—"

"Then we find Malphi."

She fixed me with a disapproving stare. "Easy as that, huh?"

I took her hand. "I'm not gonna lie to you, Sammy. Azi will fight me if I go after Malphi. It'll get messy. But that's why we're here. To try and avoid it."

She sighed and held up her wrist. "Why the hell is an archangel living on top of a mountain in New York? And why would said angel help us? I mean, he's going to know what you are right off the bat. I don't see him lending a helping hand to the enemy. How do we know he won't just try to take me like the other angel did?"

I placed a finger beneath her chin and lifted her head so that we were eye to eye. "Don't," I whispered. "Don't do that. You should know by now that there's no black and white. No discernable line between good and evil. If Heckle sent us here, then I'm sure it's safe." I almost believed the lie. "I have a demon living inside me, yet I know you'll swear with your dying breath that I'm not evil."

"That's different," she pouted.

"How so?"

"Because you're not." She jabbed a finger in the direction of the mountain. "But he won't know that."

"You have no idea what we'll find when we get to the top. For all we know, Michael is up there because he doesn't like what's going on with the others. I will not let them hurt you." I grabbed her hand and held tight. The cuff glinted in the dying sunlight. "I swear I won't let this thing take you away. Not when I just got you back."

She leveled her gaze at me, not buying what I was selling, and holy fuck was it hot. I moved closer, stopping only when our faces were inches apart. The smell of her overrode my senses, making me forget why we'd come. The closeness of her blotted out the danger hanging over our heads until it was blurred and far off. Her colors changed. She parted her lips. Her mouth pressed against mine, and I waited, breath held and heart hammering, but she didn't move. Sam stood there, leaning against me, every inch of her a humming vibration that I wanted desperately to feel in every way possible.

Her tongue slipped between my lips, so soft. So barely there. I closed my eyes and sighed. Contact. A physical connection. Sam was my lifeline to sanity. It was true what she'd said. We were more than stolen moments and forbidden touches. But I wanted her. All of her.

Her tongue skated across my bottom lip, then traced the top, tasting. The sensations were electric—the feel of her so close, the scent of her all round me. She tasted like home to me. Sam tasted like forever. Screw heaven and hell. Fuck Heckle and anyone else who stood in our way. The universe made her for me. Not for them. Not for Azirak. Not to be a pawn used to tip the balance in either direction. There would be no saving anyone who tried to remove her from my life. From my future.

It took more control than I thought I possessed, but I pulled away, hands still tangled in her hair. "Let's get moving."

The cabin Heckle told us about wasn't hard to find—a simple log shack with stacks of firewood surrounding the entire perimeter like a crude wooden fortress wall. "This is it?" Sam asked, sounding unimpressed. "I was expecting something more…"

"Grandiose?"

She laughed. "Yeah, maybe." Fingers threaded through mine, she took a deep breath. The smallest ribbon of pink, of hope, swirled around her shoulders. "Time to get this over with."

The walk up the path was strange. With each step, the temperature grew warmer. The closer we came to the shack, the more different it looked. They were subtle changes at first. The color of the wood lightened. The stacks of firewood became less defined. The overgrowth of vegetation took on hints of off-season color and changed their shape.

By the time we were halfway up the walk, the small wooden shack had transformed into a stately white manor with a perfectly trimmed lawn and blooming foliage. The snow that had coated the ground everywhere else was gone. Here, it was summer. The trees that were bare and lifeless moments ago now thrived with color and life.

Sam stopped just short of the door and surveyed the plot. "I feel like someone just slipped me some acid."

"No shit." I banged on the door. "If he answers the door in a speedo, we're out of here."

We waited, but no one appeared. I pounded again. This time the door creaked opened, but there was no one in sight.

"'Cause that's a good sign," Sam said. I started forward, but she grabbed my arm and wrenched me back. Shaking her head, she said, "Um, did you miss that movie?"

"What movie?"

"The one where the door conveniently opens, the guy walks inside, and is never heard from again?"

"What the hell movie was that?"

"I dunno," she said, rolling her eyes. "Like, every horror

movie ever made?"

"I thought it was usually a stacked blonde bouncing up the stairs in skimpy clothing when she should be running down in sensible shoes?"

"Either way," Sam said, trying to hide a grin. She hitched her thumb toward the door. "Never a good sign."

I bit back a laugh and pushed inside. Sam stayed close. I would have preferred she wait outside, but that wasn't going to happen unless I handcuffed her to the railing.

Hmm. Handcuffs.

Fuck. Mind in the game, Jax.

The hallway was long, lined with white marble and gold trim along the ceiling. Light fixtures hung down, one every eight feet or so, resembling feathers. Every so often a breeze would blow through, ruffling them and making odd shadows dance across the walls.

"Obviously the outside is, um, a little deceiving. I feel like there's a Doctor Who joke in here somewhere," Sam said. She ran her hand along the wall, tracing a circular pattern.

"Doctor *who*?"

She stopped walking and stared. "Seriously?"

"I take it I should know what that is?"

"We are officially over," she said in mock disgust. "Finished."

There was another door at the end of the hall, this one painted gold. Gaudy as hell. It, too, opened when we neared, but this time I hesitated. "Kick me to the curb later," I told her as I nudged it open a little more with the toe of my boot. The room beyond looked empty. "Right now, we need to find Michael."

"And why, might I ask, are you looking for me?"

I turned and Sam jumped, letting out a squeak. "Jesus," she said, grabbing the wall for balance.

"Nope," the man answered with an amused grin. "Though

we were BFFs back in the day."

"What is it with you people and popping out of nowhere?"

Michael stood about six feet tall, and had dark hair and a long, angular face. There was a mist around him, similar to the emotion I saw on people, only thinner and just a single color. White. He eyed me head-to-toe, then turned to Sam.

"It is strange that you should come here to seek me out, of all people, but I welcome you all the same." He gestured to the door. "Please. Come in and sit."

"It's not a social call," I said, leery. A demon shows up to your house and you invite him in for brews and bullshit? No.

"I'm quite sure it's not. Your kind would hardly partake in social activities with mine." He turned to Sam. "And it would appear you have much more interesting company."

He led the way, and we followed him into the room. Sam took a seat on the large white wraparound couch, while I stayed by the door. I didn't trust him, but I was confident that I could grab Sam and bolt if needed.

"Bel Heckle told us where to find you," she started.

"Ahh," Michael said, sitting and folding both hands in his lap. "How is Abel these days? Still trying to control the universe?"

From his tone, he and Heckle weren't on the best of terms. My hackles rose immediately. Why the fuck would he send us here if he and the archangel were in the middle of a pissing match? Then again, it seemed everyone who knew Heckle wasn't thrilled with him. Myself included.

Sam held up her hand. "I take it you know what it is?"

"I do," Michael said with a smile.

She ran a thumb over the cuff. "Heckle said you might be able to remove it?"

"There's a possibility I can help you remove it."

"A possibility," I repeated. "Either you can take it off, or not."

"Fakori cuffs are powerful. The cuff is at the mercy of the controller's will. Normally they cannot be removed by anyone other than the individual who placed them."

Every second we spent humoring this freak was another second shaved from Sam's life. "Normally, but not always?"

Sam was doing a better job keeping her cool than me. Every muscle twitched, and each nerve was on fire. Azi stirred. It didn't like Michael to begin with, and his irritating banter only made things worse. I didn't know how much longer I could keep it together.

"Yes or no?" I snapped, determined to get this moving.

"I will attempt to help you—but make no promises."

Finally. Some good news. "And what do you want in exchange?" I didn't need Heckle's warning. There was no way this was happening out of the goodness of his heart.

"You're assuming I want something. Why?"

"Nothing in life is free," I countered. I wasn't interested in playing games, and neither was Azi. "Just spit it the fuck out and get on with it."

Michael tilted his head. His eyes went from me, to Sam, then back to the cuff. "And what will you do with the Pure if the cuff is removed and her life is spared?"

"If you're asking if I plan to use her power, then the answer is no."

"I know all about you, Jax Flynn." He leaned a little closer. "And my old friend Azirak. A demon royal. Do you expect me to believe you have no intention of using the Pure to gain dominance for your side?"

"Yeah," I growled. "I do."

Michael turned to Sam, studying her. "I believe you," he said after a minute. "But the demon does not share your restraint. It will use her. And because of her love for you, she will allow it."

"I'm not on either side," Sam fired back. "I would never—"

"Aren't you?" Michael stood and began to pace. "It is obvious that you don't have a clear view of things." He stopped and turned, pinning her with a cold stare. "Not of yourself. Not of Heckle." He turned to me. "And not of *him*. Before I consider helping you, you'll have to do something for me."

I folded my arms and snorted. "Like I said…"

"I don't require a trade, demon. Not yet. I simply ask that you see the truth and understand the situation, because what happens from here is monumentally important."

"Important, how?" Sam asked. She was engrossed in the angel's words, but I wasn't fooled.

"Do you accept my proposal?"

"You haven't told us what you wanted us to do," I said, taking several steps closer to Sam.

Michael smiled, a lopsided grin that made Azi uneasy. "All I am asking is that you two observe. Watch and learn the truth."

I looked from him to Sam, then back again. He was being purposefully vague. "The truth about what?"

"Yourselves, of course."

Chapter Twelve

"Ourselves?" I looked from Michael to Jax, confused and uneasy.

The angel gave me what I supposed he considered a reassuring smile, but it was all tooth and had the opposite effect. It reminded me of Alice in Wonderland's Cheshire Cat. Full of secrets and ulterior motives. "You have questions. I can feel them. Surely you want answers."

"Just like that?" The tone of Jax's voice said he wasn't buying it, and I couldn't say I blamed him. The deeper into this we got, the less clear it became who we could trust. It seemed everyone had their own agenda. "No one else is willing to give us these answers, but you are? Bullshit."

Michael sighed. "Just like a demon. Untrusting and crass."

I caught Jax's gaze, silently pleading for him to ease up. This might be my only chance to get the cuff off. Maybe get some answers, too, like why I had been able to link us. Maybe I could figure out how to undo it before our combined emotions caused something catastrophic to happen. "What is it you want us to do?"

"Go on a journey, so to speak."

"A journey?" Jax asked, suspicion tainting his voice. "Where? We don't have time—"

"Not really a where, but a when."

"When," I repeated. Time travel? Was that what he was implying? Maybe living out here in the mountain air had short circuited his brain.

"Several whens, actually," Michael said. "In order to understand the situation in which you currently find yourself, and those who wish to control your power, you must first understand your place in the scheme of things. Both of you. You must fully understand that each choice you make from this point potentially carries the weight of the world."

The *weight of the world*? I couldn't even manage to wash the dishes or pay the cable bill on time. "And what do we have to do, exactly?"

"Simply sit down and close your eyes. I will do the rest."

I looked at Jax. Brows lowered in a scowl, he narrowed his eyes at our new friend. I knew just how he felt. I wasn't thrilled with this idea, either. But this was the condition. If we didn't do it, Michael wouldn't help us remove the cuff. If the cuff wasn't removed, it would kill me. Jax hadn't admitted it outright, but I knew. Killing Malphi would be impossible. He insisted Azi would fight him, but the truth was far worse than that—the demon would never allow its mate to be killed. That meant Chase would never take the cuff off—or worse, he'd use it as a bargaining chip like Heckle said. I could feel it, getting tighter around my skin, constricting to suffocate out everything that I was.

No. This was our best chance. And if in the process we got answers to some of the questions Heckle refused to answer? That would be a bonus. "Okay," I said. "Okay, we'll do it."

I waited for Jax to argue, but he simply took a seat next to me, the rock that he'd always been, and slipped his hand into mine.

"Now what?" he asked.

"Now," Michael said with an eerie grin. He snapped his fingers. "It's show time."

A rush of panic rose like a tidal wave inside me. Out of nowhere, my eyelids grew leaden, and I felt as though my head had gained twenty pounds. It was far too heavy to keep up. I let it fall back against the cushion, and there was a sudden flash of white before everything went dark. Moments later, the light returned, but I wasn't on the couch with Jax anymore. Michael was gone, too.

I was alone.

"Jax," I called, worry bubbling up in the pit of my stomach. "Jax, where are you?"

There was no answer. I turned in the other direction and found myself in a familiar setting. Kelly and Rick's houses sat twenty feet away, side by side, but something about them was off. Newer, I realized after a moment of staring. Less worn than they'd been yesterday. The Flynn house was the same horrible shade of mustard yellow it'd been when I'd moved in with Kelly. They'd repainted it blue when I was fourteen.

While I didn't want to move forward without Jax, the chances of me finding him standing still were slim. I hurried across the street. It was dark out, and the stars shone bright and clear from a cloudless sky. Judging from the trees and flowerbeds, it was sometime in the late spring or early summer. Next door, Kelly's rose bush was in bloom. She'd loved that smelly thing and had been crushed when the mailman backed over it six years ago.

I crept up to the Flynn house and stepped onto the porch. The door was open a few inches. I moved to slip inside, but something at the corner of the house caught my attention. A small dark haired boy was making his way into the backyard. I decided to follow.

He walked around the house, then settled on the picnic table between the two houses. I held my breath. He was looking straight ahead, but didn't seem to see me. It made me braver. I held my breath and moved closer, stopping right beside the table. To be sure, I waved my hand in front of his face. Nothing.

The little boy pulled something out of his pocket. A small green thing. A turtle. He placed it on the table, then folded both feet beneath him and looked over at the house next door. Kelly's house.

How had I not realized it right away? Jax. This was Jax. I'd never known of him having a pet turtle, though. At first I assumed it was before I'd come to live with Kelly, but movement in the window upstairs next door squashed that theory.

Jax sighed. "That's her, Harvey," he said, still looking up at the window. "Mrs. Merrick's niece. She moved in today, after they buried her parents." He looked down at the turtle as it slowly crawled across the table. "She's like me and Chase. An orphan."

The turtle got close to the edge, and Jax gingerly picked him up and set him back in the middle before resuming his inspection. "I met her today. Sorta. We didn't talk or anything. She was sad. I liked her, though. She's different. A lot like me." He sniffled then let out a long breath. "Only not bad like I am. I heard what Dad said, Harvey. That I shouldn't be allowed to live." Another sniffle.

Jesus Christ. What the hell kind of person says something like that to a child? Jax never spoke much about his parents. He said he didn't remember them, and that Rick had been the only father he'd ever known. After they'd died, he and Chase had been sent to live with Rick. The pain in his voice was far too much for a young boy, and the look in his eyes, a familiar spark of self-deprecation, made my heart hurt for him.

"I don't wanna be bad, Harvey. I want to be her friend. She's alone. I can tell. So am I," he said. Fat tears gathered in the corners of his eyes, spilling over to roll down his cheeks. "But Dad said I have to. I'm bad and I don't have a choice." He sniffled once more, then swiped his eyes with the heel of his hand. A twist of determination showed in the hitch of his lip.

He stood and climbed onto the table, taking one last look at the window of my bedroom before glancing down at the turtle crawling across the surface. It had ventured close to the edge again, so I assumed he'd pick it up and place it back in the middle of the table as he had before. Instead, he lifted his leg high. "I'm bad and I don't have a choice," he repeated, bringing his foot down hard onto the turtle. The scene was sickening. Crushing bits and a wet, *wrong* sound mingled with his crying.

I gasped, surprised by the sudden brutality of it. A second later, it all vanished.

Chapter Thirteen

"Sammy?" I tried again. No answer. If anything had happened to her, I would rip that bastard's wings out feather by feather, then cram them up his ass one at a time.

Everything had gone dark, and when I was able to see again, I was in an unfamiliar living room. There were bright red flowers on all the tables and pictures on the mantel. I picked up the one closest to the edge. A blond woman and bald man, both smiling. I'd never seen them before. I set it down and moved to the next. The same couple, still smiling, only in addition there was a small dark-haired girl. Like them she was smiling, but there was a haunted look in her large brown eyes. I would have known it anywhere.

I would have known *her* anywhere.

In the picture, Sam was several years younger than when I met her. Four, maybe five years old. I didn't know much about her parents, but seeing them together in the picture, I was struck by the lack of resemblance. From the color of her hair to the shape of her face, there was nothing similar.

"What are we supposed to do, Toni?" a man's voice said.

I turned toward the sound and found that I was no longer alone. The same couple from the pictures now sat side by side on the couch behind me.

"Nothing, Paul," the woman said. Her eyes were red-rimmed and swollen. "I had the lawyer double check the paper work. It's ironclad. There's nothing they can do to take her."

The man wasn't placated. He stood and began pacing, fingers knotted and fists shaking. "I'll kill them, Toni. If they come and try to take her back, I'll—"

"Samantha is ours," the woman insisted with conviction. The ferocity in her voice was unmistakable. "No court is going to take her away from us and give her back to those—those horrible *people*."

Sam had been adopted? Not that it mattered. Chase and I had been adopted. It never meant anything more than someone out there had cared enough to want us. To want me. Our own parents, the little I remembered about them, had been hard on me. My father, especially. I never blamed him. Somehow he'd known what I was from the start, exactly what I would become. He'd taught me to hate myself before I even truly understood what that meant.

Sam would feel the same way I did. The Merricks had wanted her. Even if I'd known nothing about them from Sam's perspective, I could see it in their eyes now. The man spoke the truth. He'd kill anyone who tried to take *his* child. And the woman, Toni, would defend her with the last breath in her body.

The scene changed. It was the same house, but the couple was nowhere in sight. The furniture was different, too. Newer. It was still night, and by the door, two tall figures crept toward the stairs.

I moved to follow, but something came out of the shadows—a man swinging a long, thin weapon that whooshed as it sliced through the air toward the intruders. One of the two men caught it and, with a laugh, ripped it effortlessly from the assailant's—Sam's father—hand. There was a scant beam of moonlight filtering through the window, and when one of the invaders stepped into it, I realized what they were. What this was.

Demons. This was it. The *home invasion* that took the life of Sam's parents and ultimately landed her in my life.

The taller of the two demons grabbed Sam's father by the throat and spun him toward the wall. "Where is the girl?" It gave a guttural snarl. "Tell me and I will let you live."

Not thinking, I rushed forward and tried to pull the demon off him. My hand went straight through it.

"What girl?" Mr. Merrick's voice was raspy as the demon's hand closed tighter around his throat. "There's no girl here."

The demon took a deep breath, then laughed. "I can smell her," it drawled. "So much energy. So *pure…*"

"How?" Sam's father stuttered. He winced as the demon pulled him back, then slammed him into the wall again. "How did you find her?"

The demon leaned closer, lips parting with a cruel smile. "The biological parents told us where to find the child, in exchange for their lives. You are being given the same opportunity. Choose wisely."

The man leveled his gaze at the demon. There was no fear in his eyes. No regret. Still trapped in the demon's grip, he drew himself up as straight as possible and said, "Do what you have to. There is no child here."

The movement was fast. A quick snap of the demon's hand and Sam's father's head rolled to the side, his eyes wide and unseeing.

"The child is upstairs. With the woman," the shorter demon

said. It led the way and I followed, wishing to hell I could do something more than simply watch this play out. What was the point of this? To show me Sam had been adopted? To tell me that her real parents were monsters for having given away her location—which, going by what I knew, seemed impossible. A Pure was undetectable until death. That's what Heckle told us.

They seemed to know exactly where to go. In one of the bedrooms, Sam's adopted mother sat on the bed with her hands folded in her lap. She portrayed a sense of calm, but her eyes betrayed her. I'd seen terror in my day—been the cause of a lot of it. There was never anything like this. I realized it wasn't for herself. She wasn't afraid of what they would do to her, but that they would find her child.

"Your husband is dead. If you don't want to follow him to the grave, tell me where the child is."

She turned, clinging to the illusion of calm, and asked, "What child?"

What followed made me sick. They tried to scare her into giving Sam up, and when that didn't work, they switched to other methods. They violated her in every way imaginable. It was brutal and senseless and even Azi wasn't interested. Through it all, she maintained her will. She refused to give up her daughter.

Through it all, I knew Sam, hidden somewhere in the room with us, watched. I'd known this had been traumatic, but it wasn't until that moment that I truly understood what she'd gone through. What it'd done to her.

The scene faded.

Chapter Fourteen

I was inside Rick's house. I would know it even with my eyes closed. It always smelled like paint thinner and tobacco, with the soft sounds of jazz drifting through the rooms. "Jax?" I tried, hoping that whatever this rollercoaster was, it would eventually bring us together. But there was no answer.

"Where's Rick?" a voice asked. I whirled around, for an insane moment thinking the child was talking to me. He wasn't, of course. He was talking to another boy. They were younger versions of Jax and Chase.

Jax shrugged. "Dunno. He said something about going to the basement."

Chase nodded and bounded down the hall. He looked to be about nine or ten.

Chase pulled open the door to the basement and peered into the darkness. "The lights are off. You sure he's down there?"

Jax walked up behind his brother. For a minute, he just

stood there, staring at Chase's back. It was like he was fighting some internal war. I saw it in his expression—the moment he decided to act. Like with the turtle, his eyes took on an eerie spark, part excitement and part regret. He raised his foot and, planting it in the middle of Chase's back, shoved with more strength than any child should have.

I didn't have time to be surprised. As Chase's shocked scream faded, the scene changed, and I was up in Jax's room. He sat on the bed, staring down at his hands. There was a knock on the door, and a moment later Rick came in.

He sat on the bed next to him. "You wanna tell me what happened?"

"I dunno," Jax said. He didn't look up from his hands, but his brows furrowed with genuine confusion. "Chase fell down the stairs."

"He had some help," Rick said.

Jax took a deep breath. Without turning to his uncle, he asked, "Is it—is he okay?"

"He's got some broken bones and a headache. Nothing life threatening. You understand this is serious though, right?"

"Dad said I was bad. He told mom I shouldn't be allowed to live."

The surprise on Rick's face was evident. Looking sick, he gritted his teeth. "He—it doesn't matter. Your dad was confused. He didn't understand you."

Jax finally lifted his head. "And you do?"

Rick smiled. It was easy in that moment to see the relationship they'd had. It must have torn Rick apart when Jax left, even though he knew there was no other choice. "Of course I do. But you need to understand something, too. You are not bad. Not even a little bit. You need to get a grip on this thing, though."

A single tear rolled down Jax's cheek. "I can't. I don't have a choice. I'm bad."

This time, Rick did raise his voice. He jumped off the bed and pulled Jax with him. "You listen to me and listen good! You are not bad. You are a little boy stuck in a horrible circumstance. You have a choice! You can choose to fight this."

"I wanted to hurt Chase," Jax said. He turned to stare out the window. A shadow passed in front of the upstairs window next door. My room. "What if I hurt her?"

Rick followed his gaze. "Who, Samantha?"

Jax nodded.

"Jax, I've seen you with Sam. You won't hurt her."

"How do you know?"

"Because Sam is your North Star, kid. You know you won't hurt her." He poked him in the chest. "Deep in here, you *know* it."

He nodded again, then turned toward the window. "I care about her."

"I know you do, and that's good. *It's good*. So you fight this for her. You make a *choice* to be good."

"I can choose to be good," Jax said as if trying to convince himself. "For Sammy."

The scene abruptly changed again. This time I was standing behind Jax. Not child-Jax, but an older Jax, yet not quite as old as he was now. This was sometime after he'd left home, I guessed. We were in a dark alley, and we weren't alone.

Jax had a man pinned against the brick wall by his throat. It was dark, but because of the streetlight overhead, I could still make them out clearly. The man struggled to breathe, his color changing from pale to reddish as he thrashed about. "You think it's funny now, fucker?"

The man clawed at Jax's hands, but made no progress. A moment later, his eyes rolled up. When his body went limp, Jax let go, and the man fell to the ground. The slight rise and fall of his chest told me he was still alive, but he'd been beaten. Badly. His lip was split in several places and both cheeks were raw. Patches of bright red decorated his arms, and thick trails of blood below his ears and nose were half dried, like this had been going on for a while. Already there were darkening bruises and places where the skin was turning purple.

Jax stood over the man, a towering figure, so vengeful and cruel. When he turned to leave, he looked right at me. He didn't see me, but I saw him. The right hand corner of his upper lip curled slightly, and there was a spark of excitement in his eyes. Of utter satisfaction. As he started forward, everything went dark.

Again the scene changed. This time I stood on the outer edge of a bedroom. It didn't look familiar, but the two people on the bed were. Jax and me. His shirt was off, as was mine, along with my jeans.

"Oh, God," I moaned, arching into him. My fingers raked across his back, and he let out a hiss of pain followed by a wicked laugh.

Despite the fact that this wasn't real, that I was merely a spectator in Michal's weird peep show, the sound sent shivers down my spine and goose bumps jumping up all over my skin. This wasn't the past. I'd only been with Jax once. The future maybe? Was it possible that Michael was showing me that there was hope for us?

Between the kisses Jax trailed down my neck, he whispered, "Just how badly do you want it, Sammy?"

The me on the bed gave another ecstasy filled moan.

"Say it," Jax demanded, nipping the flesh at the hollow of my throat. "Tell me how bad you want it. Tell me to take you."

"I—" The other me gasped as he slipped his hand into the satiny material of my panties. "No. We can't—it's…"

"We can," he insisted in a deep, seductive tone. "*We will*. Your body is giving me all the answer I need, Sammy. You want me."

"I want you," I said in a breathy whisper. "But—"

He swallowed the rest of whatever protest I was about to make with a scorching kiss. It wasn't really me being devoured by those lips, yet I felt it from the bottom of my toes, to the tips of my hair.

Another voice floated from the darkness. A hulking form, vaguely female, stepped from the shadows on the other side of the room. *"Do it,"* the thing cackled. *"Take the prize, Azirak."*

My pulse spiked, heartbeat humming through every inch of my body.

"Claim the Pure!"

I blinked. That was all. The quickest flutter of my eyelids. When I opened my eyes, all our clothes were off, and Jax was inside me. And by me, I meant *me.* I had taken vision-me's place on the bed beneath Jax.

The moment it happened, I felt it. A single moment of utter surrender was all it took. The air in my lungs froze. Solidified. The world fell away. The pain was unlike anything I'd ever imagined. A million teeth tearing at my flesh. Ten thousand dull knives digging at my skin. A scream tore from my throat, but there was no sound. There was nothing. In that moment, I stopped existing.

"Sam?"

I whirled around, losing my balance and ending up a heap on the concrete in the same spot across the street from Rick's house where I'd started. A vision. None of it had been real. Michael's sick idea of a bad joke. Still, as Jax—the real flesh and blood one this time—reached for me, I couldn't help scooting along the ground to avoid his reach.

"Sam, you're shaking. What the fuck just happened?"

He reached for me again and I scrambled to my feet, putting as much distance between us as possible. "Don't!" I forced in a breath. Yeah. Breathing was good. Necessary. "Don't… Just give me a sec."

"You're scaring me," he said. But he stayed where he was.

"I've been seeing—"

"Scenes from our past, right?" He looked worried.

"Your past, mostly," I said.

"What have you seen in my past?" There was a note in his voice that left me cold.

"Nothing I didn't already know." It wasn't a total lie. I figured the point of this was to show me that Jax wasn't the docile, warm and fuzzy person Michael assumed I thought he was. I knew all that, though. I saw Jax clearly. He wasn't a saint, but he wasn't a hell spawn, either. He was flawed, but in that imperfection lay the man I loved.

"That doesn't answer my question, Sammy." He moved in a little closer. "Was that—is that why you were near hysterical? Because of something you saw?"

"No matter what I saw, it changes nothing." And that was true. The vision wasn't real. It hadn't happened. It didn't change my feelings for him. But, it had freaked me out. There was a reason I'd been shown that, and the motivation behind it is what scared me. "If you'd just give me a min—"

"Bullshit," he snapped. "If you think—"

A rumbling noise cut him off, and the ground beneath us began to shake. Jax grabbed my arm and pulled me up, but it was too late. The concrete opened up and swallowed us whole.

Chapter Fifteen

JAX

One minute Sam and I were on the street, the next we were being choked down by the earth. It took a moment, but as my eyes got used to the dim light, I was able to see we were in someone's kitchen.

Sam stood next to me, rubbing her eyes with the heel of her hand, and to her left was…Sam. A younger version, fourteen or fifteen. She stood in front of Kelly, head bowed and shoulders rigid.

"I want the truth," Kelly screamed. "Tell me who was driving."

"I was," Sam insisted. She lifted her head, eyes meeting her aunt's with a spark of challenge. "It was me."

"What is wrong with you?" Kelly raged.

"Rick said I could pay him for the damage over time. He said—"

"Do you think I'm a fool?" her aunt demanded, dropping her voice. "That I don't know who was really driving?"

"It wasn't—"

Kelly slapped her. The sound echoed through the room, and even though the moment was long gone, I was still furious. This was the aftermath of the night I'd crashed Rick's car. Sam and I had both been drinking, and I'd been an asshole, insisting I was fine to drive. A deer ran out in front of the car, and I swerved to miss it but ended up veering into a tree. Sam made me switch places before the police arrived, telling them it'd been her behind the wheel. I'd already been in so much trouble. One more strike would have landed me in an entirely new pot of hot water.

"You told me she was pissed, but that it was no big deal," I said as calmly as I could manage. "She hit you, Sammy. She fucking hit you."

Sam ignored me, watching the scene unfold.

"You're going to let him ruin your life, Samantha," Kelly barked. "The police chief says this will go on your permanent record. For what? To protect some loser who will knock you up the first chance he gets and then leave you hanging?"

Kelly had always hated me, and I couldn't give a shit, but I'd never heard such venom directed at Sam before.

"I did what I had to do," the Sam beside me said softly, looking away from the scene. "You can't fault Kelly. She never knew you like I do."

I didn't get the chance to respond. The room changed again, this time dumping us out in an open field. Michael stood in the shadow of a large tree, arguing with another man.

"You cannot do this," said the one I didn't know. He placed a hand on Michael's shoulder. "It will tear our kind apart."

"It is already done," Michael said, brushing the other's hand away. "The inequality is unacceptable, Gabriel. It ends now."

"Angels," Sam whispered. She stepped around me and

walked toward them, enthralled by their presence. "But if we've been seeing things from *our* past, why show us this?"

I shrugged and joined her closer to where they stood. "Who the hell knows? This whole thing is a mind fuck, if you ask me. That bastard doesn't know anything about getting that thing off your wrist. We need to cut our losses and go find—"

"Shh." She waved at me and leaned closer to the arguing pair.

"What brought this about, brother?" Gabriel took a step back and shook his head. "Things are as they have been for eons."

"Exactly," Michael said. "We will fight for our right to be more than just drones. To matter."

Gabriel took a step back, stunned. "This will lead to exile."

"Then so be it," Michael said, resolute.

Everything grew blurred and watery. I thrust my hand out, blindly searching for Sam, but caught nothing but air. When it all cleared, I was someplace else, thankfully with Sam beside me.

"Now what?" she said, glancing around. We were outside in the middle of a thicket. Several men approached from a distance.

I took her hand and pulled her from the path. "No choice. We wait it out."

There were four of them, Michael at the front. Not humans, but angels. They stopped a few feet from us as two more came from the other direction to meet them.

"Is it true?" One of the two asked. He was tall with blond hair and a thin mustache.

Michael nodded and bowed his head. "I am afraid so. We are exiled. Fallen from His grace."

The rest said nothing, but there was a profound sadness in the air. Despite the fact that none of this was real, it stirred the demon, making Azi rumble with hunger.

"We must find a Pure," Michael continued. "If we kill it and claim its energy, then we will have the power to go home."

Again the area changed. This time Sam and I stood in front of...Sam. Another her, anyway. And another me. We were as we were today, even dressed in the same clothing. Sam stood between Michael and me. She was backlit by an unyielding glow, and both Michael and I had one of her wrists in our hands, playing tug of war.

On my side, the glow around her changed red, while on Michael's side, it turned brighter and whiter. "Okay," the real Sam said, stepping closer and squinting against the light. "Out of everything, this makes the least sense."

"It makes perfect sense. Don't you get it?" I turned away from the vision and grabbed her hands. "Heaven and hell fighting over you. Tearing you apart to use for their own ends."

A small noise escaped her throat, her skin paling. Vision Sam's eyes popped open. She jerked from Michael's and my grasp like it was nothing, bringing her hands to wrap around each of our necks. Throwing back her head, she let out an unworldly howl, and as we watched, both Michael and I turned to ash.

Sam was quiet for a moment. The expression on her face lingered between surprise and terror. "What the hell was that supposed to mean?"

"I dunno, but there's something I need to tell you," I said, not really wanting to continue. She needed to know. Deserved to know. The problem was, I knew that after she found out the truth, she'd see her parent's death as *her fault*. But I'd seen it for a reason. Her parentage must have had some significance. "A few of the things I saw—" Shit. How was I supposed to spit this out?

"Saw?"

"I don't think the Merrick's were your parents." Smooth, asshole. Real smooth. "Not biologically."

She shook her head and laughed. "No way. You must have misunderstood. Of course they're my parents."

The light faded and the vision Michael, Sam, and me disappeared, leaving us alone. "I saw them talking. They were afraid your real parents would try to take you back."

She shook her head, grin fading. "I would know if that were true."

"I'm afraid it *is* true," Michael said. He was in front of us now, arms folded and mouth set in a grim line.

Sam opened her mouth, then closed it for a moment. Holding up her hand, she said, "I'm assuming we did what you wanted. Can you tell me how to remove this now?"

"Not just yet," Michael said. "I need to know you understand the gravity of your situation."

"The gravity?" Sam screamed. Her colors swirled, a mix of red and black. "I think the gravity of 'if you don't get this cuff off you'll die' is pretty damn clear."

"You are not simply Pure," Michael said, ignoring her outburst. "Among your kind, you are special. Rare."

Were these assholes incapable of giving straight answers? "Rare? What does that mean?"

The archangel shook his head, hesitating for a minute before continuing. "Sam is a special kind of Pure. In fact, I don't know that there has ever been one like her before."

"What makes me so special?"

"With the purified soul of two Pure parents, she is unique. That is multiplied by the fact that she died and lives again, and also because she is the last in her line."

"Last in my line? But what if I have a child? You said this runs for generations. Why wouldn't it be Pure?"

"Your birth parents destroyed both their lines, ending each with you."

"How—" Sam was confused, and I didn't blame her. She still didn't know the whole story.

"They told the demons where to find you," I supplied. Turning to Michael, I added, "That's what did it, isn't it?"

Michael nodded. "That crime dissolved the last of the purified soul in both of them, and nullified future generations."

"They told—why would they do that?" Sam took a step away from us and ran both hands through her hair. The murky colors swirling around her head grew bolder and bleaker. "And my parents—the Merricks. It was me. They died because of me…"

Michael frowned. "Your birth parents are responsible for the deaths of the Merricks—not you. Since there is no way for a demon, or an angel for that matter, to tell which human souls are Pure until they die, they needed help. Without them, the demons would have never found you as a child, Sam."

"But they were Pures themselves," Sam said, confused. "And they were obviously still alive, so how did the demons find *them*?"

He shook his head slowly. "They knew what they were. In life, as a Pure grows, they have a predilection toward either good or evil. I'm sad to say, your parents leaned toward the darker side of their nature. They sought out the demons and offered to sell your location"

Sam looked sick. "But why would they do that?"

"Money, power—the exact nature of the exchange is unknown to me."

"So the Merricks sacrificed their lives to keep me hidden," she whispered. "And it was all for nothing."

"You shouldn't look at it like that." The angel's voice softened, and for a second, he looked as though he felt sorry for her. "Paul and Toni Merrick enabled you to survive into adulthood. That's no small feat for your kind. They gave you a chance to grow and become someone who could take care of herself."

"Yep." Sam threw her hands into the air. "And then I

went and essentially killed myself, undoing everything. Just awesome."

"Yes," Michael said. "Now you're as bright as the sun to both angels and demons. But remember that there is always a choice. Heaven and hell want to use you, but because you have been activated, they cannot do so without your consent."

Sam laughed. "Well then, problem solved. I'm not consenting to shit."

"Ah, but it's more complicated than that." He began to pace. "The reason I showed you the things I did was so that you would understand. Choices are not something always made as freely as it would seem. There are outside influences, connections and attachments to take into consideration, small, unseen nudges—"

Sam's skin grew pale, and I reached for her hand. "What? What am I missing?"

"Something I saw," she said softly.

This. This was the thing that had her so messed up when I'd found her.

"Yes," Michael said with a sigh. "To be claimed, the agreement need not be verbal. It simply has to be implied. Taking the bond between you and Jax into consideration, you must be fully aware of the possible outcome of your actions. All of them."

"What the hell is he talking about?" I whirled on Sam.

She ignored me, still focused on Michael. "That's why Heckle made the deal he did with Jax. It's why we can't be together. Because we could accidentally…"

Again Michael nodded. "I imagine so."

"Then that would mean he knew." Around her shoulders, a swirl of red exploded into the air, so dense that it nearly blotted her from my sight entirely. "He made it seem like my coming back *activated* was a surprise. But it couldn't have been. Not if he made the deal before it even happened!"

And then I understood what she was saying. Like a bolt of lightning striking me down, so many things made sense. The almost primal need I had for Sam. The nearly uncontrollable, dark desire to possess her any way I could.

"Let me make sure I have this straight," I said with as much calm as I could muster. Azi stirred in a mix of excitement and fury, and I tamped it down. A spike of jealousy, mixed with the sting of Heckle's betrayal hung like a noose around my neck. "You're saying that to claim a Pure, an angel or demon would need to—"

"No, no," Michael said. "But the intimate relationship, coupled with the intensity of your feelings for each other, could easily allow her to be claimed during…a moment of passion. Azirak could manipulate the situation."

"Well, then we won't be crossing that line." Sam looked like she might throw up. I knew how she felt.

"You must not." The archangel's expression was all pity, and I had the urge to wipe it away using the sole of my boot. "Because should either side get hold of you, it would not be long before you consented. Temptation would be their first attempt—which is why your relationship is dangerous. The next step would be far less pleasant. The human mind cannot fathom the depths of torture available to us."

"If that's a threat…" I stepped in front of Sam, letting the rest of the sentence linger between us. "In that fucked up vision quest you just sent Sam and me on, you showed us that you needed someone like Sam to go *home*. If you think I'm going to let you—"

"Like the demons, some of the angels were cast out as well. I among them." His lips pulled downward. "Like Lucifer, I started a rebellion, though not to the same extent. I, and about twenty others, were banished from heaven, doomed to walk the earth for ten thousand years."

"And?"

"And, if you're asking me if I plan to use Sam to get back into heaven, the answer is no."

"Why?" she asked. "Not that I'd be a willing volunteer, but if I'm the way for you to get back, then why not do it?"

"I've been here a long time. I see that I was wrong in challenging God's will. I accept my fate and will not fight my punishment. But the others are not quite so resolved. They feel their comeuppance was too severe."

Sam seemed to think about this for a moment before taking a deep breath. "Okay, so what was the point in showing us all that crap?"

"As I said, you needed to understand certain things in order to make a choice"

"Choice?" Sam said. "What choice?"

"How long do you think it will be before one side or the other finds you? How long do you believe you can keep running?" He took a deep breath. "I can smell the link. It *will* be your undoing."

"I'll protect her," I said, as Azi flashed an image of me facing off against the armies of heaven and hell to keep Sam safe. Then, in another flash, it stood side by side with the cloaked female demon, each holding a chain wrapped around Sam's neck. "Just get the damn cuff off so we can be on our way."

"I'm sorry. That won't be possible."

"What?" Sam and I both exclaimed. She looked from him to her arm. "But you said—"

"I said I would help you. And I will. I cannot remove the cuff, but under the right circumstance, one of you can."

"You bastard!" Sam started forward, but I grabbed her arm and dragged her back.

"I mean you no harm, and I do not wish to see you fail in your quest, but you must understand something. Despite what the bible, Heckle, or anyone else tells you, free will is an illusion. You humans are free, but you're nothing more than pawns laid out on a chessboard between good and evil. Heaven and hell. You think the moves you make are your own, but really, you're being nudged and twisted for millions of otherworldly purposes."

"I don't believe you," Sam said, shaking her head slowly.

"No? Heckle is all the proof you need. He tricked you. He knew all along what would happen if he returned the Pure soul to your body."

"Then why do it?" I challenged. From what I knew of Heckle, it went against everything he stood for. "He said it unbalanced things."

"I believe he sees it as a means to an end. You take it far too personally. More than likely, Heckle did what he did to right an imbalance. I imagine he already knows how this will end. Who will claim you."

Sam jerked out of my grasp and stalked forward. Inches from Michael's face she said, "No one is claiming me."

Michael fixed a pitying frown on her. "It is inevitable. There's no place for you to hide now."

I stepped between them. "Not going to happen."

"I suppose only time will tell." He leveled his gaze at me and I fought back the urge to lash out. "I think you would be surprised at the kind of motivation that comes with her kind of power. I imagine after twenty-four hours of torture, most humans would agree to anything."

Michael snapped his fingers. There was a weight in the room, followed by an echoing clap as darkness settled over us. The absence of light, of sound, was nearly crushing. But just as fast as it began, it was over. When it lifted, we were back outside the cabin.

I scanned the area around and sighed. "Guess he's done with us."

Chapter Sixteen

SAM

We were back on the steps, the huge white house again in its original, shack-like form. I let out a frustrated scream. The sound bounced off the trees and echoed through the woods with eerie resonance.

"Feel better?" Jax, unfazed by my uncharacteristic outburst, took my hand and tugged me down the steps.

"No," I replied, following. We'd just wasted a chunk of time and were still sitting on square one. One of us could remove the cuff under the right circumstance? What the hell was that supposed to mean? If at all possible, Michael was even more cryptic than Heckle — and that's something I didn't think could happen. "Now what?"

"We're running out of time. I'm not sure we have a choice anymore." He glared down at my wrist and then back at me, studying my face with concern. "How do you feel?"

I flexed my fingers. Pins and needles shot up my arm, all the way to my shoulder. My hand was cold, like I'd been keeping it submerged in ice water. And every once in a while the cuff would constrict, sending a deep, throbbing pain rippling throughout my entire body.

"I'm tired," was my response. "That doesn't necessarily mean it's the cuff. It's been a long day."

Jax didn't answer. Instead we started back down the mountain. I wasn't sure how long we'd been inside Michael's freaky *blast-from-the-past*, but the moon was high in the sky and the temperature had dropped.

The car came into sight before Jax spoke again. "I'll do whatever I have to, Sammy. You know that, right?" He stopped walking as we cleared the path, and grabbed both my hands.

I knew he meant it, but that wasn't the issue. It wasn't just the two of us involved in this. There was a third party to consider. One with more pull than either one of us wanted to admit. "I know. But you need to consider the alternative."

He pushed me away and closed the distance between him and the car.

"Jax." I followed.

"Don't." He yanked open the door and threw himself into the driver's seat. "Whatever defeatist crap you're going to spout, just save it."

Somewhere in the world pigs were cleared for takeoff and cats were dating mice. Jax was being the positive one?

I slid into the passenger's seat and closed the door. As he stomped on the gas pedal, I said, "I'm going to ask you a question. Just one, and then I won't bring it up again. Tell me the truth."

"Okay."

"Are you one hundred percent sure that you can take out Malphi?"

Without looking my way, he let his lips twist in a grin made of his trademark confidence. "Of course I—"

"That's not what I mean." I swallowed the lump forming in my throat. "Are you certain that Azirak will *let* you take Malphi out?"

He clenched his jaw and gave the car more gas. We lurched forward and took the next turn fast. What bothered me most wasn't his silence, but the feeling of utter despair I felt radiating from the link.

Jax pulled over about three miles into Harlow. We'd driven all night and made great time, but hadn't said much to each other during the trip. In all fairness, I slept a chunk of the way. I was tired and my muscles had begun to ache. The chill that had been confined to my hand now seemed to have spread outward, enveloping both arms, my chest, and the right side of my neck.

It was a little after nine in the morning. I stretched and shifted in the seat as Jax killed the engine. For some reason he'd pulled into a park and ride on the edge of Flossmoor camping grounds.

He didn't say a word as he undid his seat belt and threw open the driver's side door. "Jax?"

No answer.

He slammed the car door and started for the woods. I fumbled with my own belt and hurried after him.

He must have walked a half mile into the brush before stopping beside a large boulder. Running his hands through his hair, he stalked back and forth in front of the rock, the gleam in his eyes so much more than haunted. Pausing, he threw back his head and let out a roar that was about as far from human as you could get.

"Jax..." I said again. I took a step toward him, then froze. His eyes flickered black for several seconds before returning to their normal, stormy gray. "Please."

"What?" His voice was laced with acid, razor sharp and full of fury. "I can feel the demon fighting me, Sammy. It—"

I grabbed either side of his face and tilted his head down so that I could look him in the eye. "So? Fight back. It's what you do—what *we* do. Focus. Focus on me."

His breathing, which had been harsh and uneven, stilled. With a flurry of movement and a barely audible growl, I was off the ground and pinned against a large pine tree a few feet away. Jax's hands on either side of my shoulders trembled slightly. "That's a bad idea." His eyes flashed again. Black. Gray. Black. Gray. They settled on a gray center rimmed in thick black. "Focusing on you unsettles us both."

He leaned into me, nuzzling my neck with the tip of his nose. I wrapped my legs tight around his waist. There was a sharp inhalation followed by a warm puff of breath and the smallest nick as he nibbled my ear. Under normal circumstances, I'd be able to see the precarious balance we were literally tripping over. I was standing at the boarding gate for a permanent vacation, for Christ's sake. But these circumstances weren't normal. They weren't even manageable. I was a slave to my emotions. To his. And right then, the vibes he was giving off were heady and undeniable.

Still, I tried. "The cuff," I rasped, as his lips brushed my collarbone and my toes just about curled. "Malphi—"

One of his hands came up to close around my neck. The pressure was firm, but not to the point where air was impossible. But the look in his eyes, now blacker than they'd been, replaced the heat and chased a cold shiver down my back. "—is none of your concern. As you, Samantha Merrick, are none of hers." For an instant Jax's fingers tightened, closing off my airway. Azi. The demon was in control. I panicked and thrashed. The reaction seemed to please it. When it released its hold, Azi wore a wicked grin. "He will never admit it, but my human likes that. The taste of your fear. He craves it in the darkest parts of his soul."

The demon pushed into me, letting go of a guttural growl.

I couldn't help it. I whimpered. Good sense told me to scream at the top of my lungs and hope to God that there was someone nearby.

"I could take you now. I am within my rights to claim you..." It brought Jax's lips back to my ear, and this time when the demon moved in, I cried out, sure that teeth had broken through the skin. "...in every way possible. Let me show you how a true demon *fucks.*"

"Please," I said, barely above a whisper. A pathetic protest, but all things considered, a win. "The cuff... It's killing me."

Azi murmured against the sensitive skin of my neck, words I didn't understand. Shifting back just enough so that I could see Jax's eyes, still so black, it whispered, "Allow me to remove it. Let me take you and—"

A dizzying oscillation from gray to black. With his lip curling upward, Jax's hand tangled through his hair and pulled savagely at the roots, as if trying to yank the demon from his body. With another bellow, he pulled away from me and sank to his knees.

I landed hard on the ground then stumbled upward, putting some distance between us. Just in case.

"I think...Sammy..." He lifted his head as his fingers knotted in the material of his T-shirt, above his heart. "I can't..."

The change was complete. Like someone had held a dropper of ink up to his eyes, they clouded over, blackening throughout, and stayed that way. The demon's gaze traveled over me, the scrutiny with which it examined me would have made me hot as hell if it had been Jax. "The sand in your hourglass is nearly drained. The cuff must come off. Now."

Some of the tension left me. "I know."

The demon said nothing as it rose, but continued to stare. Black eyes were hungry, and every few moments, it looked like it was trying to hold back. Like it wanted to finish what it had started a few moments ago.

"There's only one way that's going to happen," I prompted softly.

The expression on Jax's face remained unchanged. "You wish to trade your life for Malphi's."

It was my turn to remain silent.

Azi sighed—an act that was so Jax, and yet so alien.

"You would have me destroy my mate in favor of my human's." It took a step toward me.

It wasn't a question and I had no idea what to say.

Another step. "I *could* do it," it said, placing a finger beneath my chin and lifting my head.

Under Azi's control, Jax's lips brushed mine. Soft at first. A barely-there tease. Then, a second later, more aggressive. His hand snaked around to the back of my neck, and with a sudden jerk, the demon pulled me flush against him. Tongue skating along my bottom lip, it paused for a moment before nipping hard. I gasped and Azi chuckled. Jax's voice, yet different. Darker and inhuman. Confusion settled over me. It wasn't Jax in control, but it was his body pressed against me. It was still him that teased the heat to my skin.

With a single, powerful thrust of Jax's hips, the demon ground his body against me, then pulled away. "But I will not."

The heat that threatened to ignite me just seconds ago fizzled, leaving only ice in its wake. "Will not what?" I asked.

"I will not trade Malphi's life for yours." Azi tilted Jax's head as though listening to something only it could hear. "My human is angry."

"Can't say I blame him," I mumbled, taking a step away. My voice wobbled and I fought to maintain control over the emotions raging inside me—everything from the most profound terror to unparalleled rage over his admission. "I'm fairly annoyed, too."

The movement was quick. One moment the demon was standing in front of me, the next it was behind me, the fingers of Jax's hand wound tight around a chunk of my hair. "I believe you misunderstand," it whispered at my ear. Warm breath tickled my neck. "I will not trade Malphi's life for yours, and I will not trade your life for Malphi's."

I wanted to move away. Unfortunately, the iron grip held me securely in place. Jax's lips skimmed the side of my neck, then worked their way across my cheek. The demon let out a contented sigh. "I will not see either of you perish."

Okay. Not what I'd expected, but still not hopeful. "It's not going to work that way." I held up my wrist and gave it a good shake. "This needs to come off. The only way that's going to happen is if Chase gets what he wants. So, yeah. One of us has to die."

Azi leaned a little closer. "Possibly not."

I didn't want to get my hopes up—I was talking to a demon after all—but I couldn't help it. "What does that mean?"

It pulled away and turned me around, and with a grin that looked so misplaced on Jax's face said, "There is a chance someone else can remove the Fakori cuff."

I snorted. We'd heard that before. "Michael said Jax or I could remove it under the right circumstance, but we have no idea what the hell those are. If that's what you're talking about, then I'm all ears."

"A descendant of the creator may also remove the cuff."

"A descendant?" I repeated. "Of Fakori?"

"Yes," was all it said.

"Well, tell me where to find him and give Jax back the steering wheel. The clock is ticking."

"I have a condition, Samantha Merrick."

Ding, ding ding. There it is. "The answer is no."

"I have not asked yet." It was eerie the way the demon stood there just watching me, his only movement the slightest flutter of Jax's eyelids.

"I already know what you want. The same thing Chase does. The same thing the angels do." I leaned closer, pinning him with what I hoped was my best intimidating glare. "The same thing your demonic bitch wants."

"Your power, you mean."

I folded my arms and shook my head. "Not going to happen."

"While your power would please my clan and enable my victory, it is not what I ask."

That surprised me. "What then?"

"Until the cuff is removed, I retain complete control over the human's body."

Chapter Seventeen

JAX/AZIRAK

"Not a chance," Sam cried. She took a menacing step forward, then hesitated and moved back several feet. "It's not gonna happen."

I opened my mouth to protest—no fucking way was I riding shotgun in my own damn body—but of course no sound came. The demon was amused by my anger, though. I felt it.

"Come to terms with the inevitable," it said. "This is your only option."

I realized the demon wasn't talking to Sam. It was addressing me. And it had a point. Without offing Malphi, Chase wouldn't remove the cuff—and that was assuming the bastard kept his word at all. And Azi had already announced it wouldn't let me kill its mate. Letting Sam die was out of the question. Since my biggest obstacle was technically living in the same body as me, this was the only path.

Fine. You get control, but only until you do what needs to be done. And so help me, you hurt her in any way, I'll take us both out.

The demon chuckled. "My human agrees."

"Bullshit," Sam spat. "I'm just supposed to believe you? Jax would never let you take over."

"He knows that your survival will only be possible through cooperation."

"Sounds like blackmail to me."

More amusement from Azirak. It held out my hand to Sam. "I am allowing him to remain conscious. He will have the ability to...keep an eye on things."

Sam hesitated then after a moment sighed. A spark of sad acceptance in her eyes made me think she felt guilty, and I wanted to set her straight. Giving the demon control was like sacrificing a piece of myself. A small part of me that, up until now, had been mine alone, untainted by the thing that lived inside me. What I wanted her to know was that I didn't care. It was worth it to me.

She was worth it.

S am had been behind the wheel for almost two hours. Her shoulders were beginning to slump, and her eyes kept drooping. *She needs to rest,* I said to Azi. *Make her pull over and you drive.*

Azi shifted my body toward her. "Pull over," it demanded.

When she didn't respond, a wave of anger erupted, and the demon latched on to the wheel, yanking it hard to the right. Sam screamed as the car jerked hard sideways. She slammed the breaks, bringing the vehicle to an uneven stop on the side of the highway.

"What the hell are you doing?"

"I commanded you to pull over," it said.

"I'm not one of your demons," she snapped. "You don't get to *command* me to do jack shit."

Her words annoyed the demon, but it didn't respond. Instead it studied her intently.

Watching Sam from Azi's perspective was strange. Since embracing the demon, all my senses had been heightened. But with Azi in control, my vision was even sharper. More detailed. Each strand of her hair had multiple layers, with millions of different colors all blended to make perfection. Her lips, slightly parted with the right corner pulled up slightly in irritation, were composed of thousands of superfine strands of color—reds, pinks, and just a hint of blue. In fact, her entire body was a beacon of assorted colors, all shifting slightly from dark to light, oscillating between degrees. She was brightness and beauty personified, from the top of her head right down to the soles of her shoes. Every place except a small section of her chest above her heart.

The small area was muddled, a lot like the murky swirl emanating around her—jumbled and dark.

The demon chuckled and Sam snorted. "Something amusing about that?"

"My human," Azi responded. "He finds your appearance disconcerting."

"My appearance?"

Don't fucking say it like that!

Of course the bastard ignored me. It ignored her, too, getting out of the car and coming around the front. With an agitated jerk, Azi pulled open her door and said, "Out."

"Out? Why would I—"

The demon's impatience grew. It grabbed Sam's arm and hauled her unceremoniously from the seat. She stumbled sideways, catching herself just before losing her balance. "I will drive. You will sleep."

"Sleep," she shouted. "How the hell do you expect me to

sleep?" Sam adjusted her jacket and stalked toward Azi. Giving him a shove, she added, "I know this whole 'living on planet Earth' thing is new for you, but let's get one thing straight. I'm not leaving you alone with him for a single minute."

She doesn't trust you, I told it.

This confused the demon for some reason. It didn't understand her tone, or the rigid set of her shoulders. It was puzzled by her expression and the volume of her voice. A rush of images bombarded my mind. Sam and I, the first time we were together. The scene played out as though I was a third party watching from the outside. It focused on the times where my eyes were dark. When the demon was in control.

"You find me repelling." A statement. Not a question.

Sam snorted. "You're basically blackmailing us. Damn right I find you *repelling*!"

"I am not hurting my human." The confusion faded, replaced by a rush of logic. Azirak really didn't see the problem here.

Sam stomped her foot. She stalked forward, bringing her face inches from mine. "*Jax*," she spat. "He's not your human. He's Jax."

There was a long moment of hesitation before the demon stepped away from her. My head nodded slowly, and the demon repeated, "Jax." It opened the car door and gestured for her to get inside. "We should go. Time runs out."

For a minute, I was sure Sam would turn and walk the other way. She had that look about her. Eyes narrow and lips pressed in a hard line, it was the expression she wore just before engaging in a fight. But she surprised me. With a sigh, she pushed past the demon and slid into the passenger seat, slamming the door behind her.

"She is an unusual human," the demon said as it moved my body around the car. Pausing with my hand on the handle, it added, "It is not surprising that you find her alluring."

Don't get any ideas, I growled. I was tempted to push for control, to fight the demon and take back what was rightfully mine, but Azi turned to look at Sam. Beneath all the vibrant colors, she was pale. The distorted mass over her heart seemed bigger than it had before, and her posture was slumped. That cuff needed to come off and we only had a short time left to do it. *You better not be bullshitting us. Find Fakori's ancestor and get that fucking thing off her.*

"I will do as I promised," it said out loud.

Sam, not realizing the demon was talking to me, huffed and shifted in her seat. She yanked the seat belt out and jammed it into the lock, then turned to face the window. "You better."

We drove for several hours. Sam dozed in and out. Azi kept our speed at a maximum of five miles an hour above the limit. Its reasoning was that we didn't want to waste time with the authorities. And while I agreed, the fact that we weren't moving as fast as possible pissed me off.

This was the longest I'd spent as a spectator. I had no love for the demon, but could almost understand its anger. I felt helpless. Weak. I was caged, and everything, even the simplest things like scratching an itch or shifting around in my seat, was beyond my control.

"I probably should have asked this up front," Sam said after a while. "But how is it that you know exactly where to find this guy?"

"I have an entire clan eagerly awaiting my return. I had but to ask, and they fell in line."

"What does that tell me?" she fired back.

"While you were sleeping I called my clan. They are searching for the Fakori descendant as we speak."

Sam looked from me to her wrist and grimaced.

I wasn't the only one who noticed. "Does it pain you?"

She didn't answer right away, and when she did, it wasn't to answer his question. "Can he hear us? Jax, I mean?"

"Of course. I gave my word. He is able to oversee our journey."

She sighed. "No. It doesn't hurt."

The demon studied her for a moment then let out a growl. "What is the purpose of that?"

"Of what?"

"Of attempting to deceive him?"

Sam snorted. "I'm not—"

"Do not lie to me!" Azirak bellowed. My body shook with a flash of anger. It was potent. The sting of it flooded what little sense I had and momentarily blocked out what was going on in the car.

"Fine," Sam snapped. "It hurts like hell." She made a fist and slammed it against the dash. The sound of it echoed through my body, the demon's heightened senses making it seem like a bomb had gone off inside my skull. "It feels like something is trying to squeeze my hand off with a pair of bolt cutters. Oh. And my body temperature? Dropping lower than a frat boy's IQ. This thing is killing me. Why don't I want Jax to know? Maybe because he's got enough to deal with right now, what with you hijacking his body, his brother trying to end the world—oh, and your demonic bitch looking for a hookup."

The demon seemed to consider her words for a moment. "I have lived a thousand lives and I still do not understand humans."

"What's not to understand?" Sam asked. Her voice softened a little. I knew the tone. Irritation blended with sympathy. "When you love someone, you want to keep them from pain."

"Demons do not love like humans. The word does not

exist within our vocabulary." A long, deep breath filled my body. "Yet I do not like that you are in pain."

"That makes two of us." She shifted around so that she was sitting sideways, facing me. "If we can find this guy, this relative of Fakori, and he can get the cuff off, then what? You'll hand Jax's body back over?"

"I said I would."

"Just like that?"

"Unlike Zenak, I am honorable. A downfall, my clan says."

"And me?"

"What of you?"

"You're going to simply hand Jax back his body and let him walk away with a Pure?"

"Samantha Merrick, the hum—*Jax*—will never be able to walk away with you. I will always be present."

"I mean, you're not going to claim me?"

The demon chuckled. It was my voice, but it wasn't. "Would you let me?"

"Nope," was her reply. "But that hasn't seemed to stop everyone else from trying."

"While your power would be an asset to my clan's cause, I am able to see what the others cannot."

"And that is?"

"Going home will serve no purpose right now."

"But it will someday?"

"There is something you need to remember, Samantha Merrick. I am, and always will be, a demon. Despite whatever human-tainted feelings I may have for you, I am dangerous."

Sam's face filled my vision, her expression a mix of surprise and fear.

As if the universe was enforcing Azi's words, everything shifted. There was a deafening sound—shattering glass and the scream of twisting metal.

Sam's cries of terror echoed through my head.

Chapter Eighteen

One minute I was staring into the face of the demon-infested guy I loved—the next, my entire world was spinning out of control.

I was beginning to notice a disturbing pattern.

I called for Jax, but it was drowned out by the cacophonous sound coming from all around us. My stomach lurched and my body was momentarily weightless as my hair obscured my vision. There was no up or down because the earth seemed to have disappeared, allowing gravity to use us as toys.

With the seat beneath me gone, my limbs flailed wildly in every direction, desperate to find something solid, a small bit of unmovable reality to prove this wasn't all just part of some horrible waking nightmare.

Then, just when I thought I'd lose my mind, my breath hitched and something crushed my body. Two ironclad limbs enveloped me as a series of breakneck crashes rattled the car.

I let go of another scream as the car gave one final

shudder, skidding to a stop in a symphony of cringe-inducing squeals and broken bits. My head slammed against something. The door. A broken seat. Hell, it could have been the steering wheel. When I opened my eyes, nothing was where it should have been.

Jax's arms, still presumably under the demon's control, loosened. "Are you well, Samantha Merrick?"

Was I well?

Whatever it was that had just happened, I was pretty damn sure *well* wasn't in the description. I shifted, moving away a few inches, and gasped. The windshield was gone, leaving only bits of jagged glass dotting the pane. The dashboard was in pieces, the large chunk in front of me buckled like tin foil.

I opened my mouth—to say what, I had no idea—but suddenly I was moving. Jax's arms tightened and a wave of vertigo hit me as a pounding noise filled the space around us. I was jostled from side to side several times, and seconds later cool air washed over me as Azi extracted me from the car and set me down on the grass outside.

"What happ—" The rest of my sentence was lost as the ground beneath my feet took a massive twist to the right.

Something heavy crashed into me from behind. An otherworldly growl split the air, followed by a series of grunts. The weight on top of me shifted and was gone. I pushed onto my knees and crawled to the shelter of a large pine then turned to see the wreckage.

Rick's car was destroyed. The fact that I was sitting here, still breathing and in possession of all my limbs, was nothing short of a miracle. But that wasn't our only problem. Just past the twisted metal, Jax's body, presumably with Azirak still behind the wheel, faced off with three angels. He stood between me and them, a fearsome vision of destruction and darkness.

"If you want the Pure, you will have to go through me."

One of the angels laughed. He was the shortest of the three, with deep red wings tipped in orange. He eyed me, gaze sweeping every inch with an almost lecherous gleam. "I will do so with pleasure, beast."

Like someone flipped the crazy switch, Azi and the angels sprang forward. It was a mass of mangled limbs, flying feathers, and bloody appendages. I'd seen Jax fight. It never failed to take my breath away. His ferocity and grace were mesmerizing. His pure power and raw strength a thing of wonder. It was nothing compared to watching Azi with full control.

The demon tore through the first angel with ridiculous ease, twisting her head with a jerk then punching a hole through her sternum for good measure. She fell to the ground as the next one stepped up. Enraged at his comrade's defeat, he let out a scream that chased a chill up my spine.

The angel's gaze swiveled in my direction for a moment before fixating on Jax. His lip curled upward, a sinister smile spreading like poison across his face. "You will not gain this power."

Azi growled, a sound so possessive, so threatening, it was a wonder the angel didn't turn tail and run. He dove for our attacker, grabbing him and hefting his body into the air. The angel roared, it's dark green wings unfurling in a furious burst. It bucked and thrashed, but was no match for the demon's strength. With a ferocious thrust, Azi lifted the angel high, then brought him down across Jax's knee with brutal force. The sound it made was sickening, and I swallowed back the bile bubbling up my throat as he let the lifeless corpse fall to the grass at his feet.

The last angel, the short one with the attitude bigger than Texas, stepped forward. His grin went from ear to ear. "My brethren were noble but weak. No match for you. Not like me."

If it were Jax standing there, he would have laughed. Maybe made some snarky quip about size. Not Azirak. He snarled, lip pulled back to bare his teeth, and pounced. It was over almost as soon as it began. The angel made a move to grab hold of Jax's throat, but his fingers never touched skin. Azi brought Jax's hands up and with a violent twist, broke the creature's neck.

As his body fell, I swallowed back another mouthful of bile and climbed to my feet. We were well off to the side of a rarely traveled road and couldn't necessarily call for a tow truck. Besides having no money, there were three dead bodies laying a few feet from Rick's mangled car. Getting rid of them would be time consuming, and leaving them would be a tough one to explain. Spending time with Jax had made me a better liar, but I wasn't that good. The car the angels had rammed us with was in slightly better condition, but a quick survey of the damage revealed two busted front tires. We were going to have to hoof it.

I gestured to the road. "Shall we?"

And we were off.

With each step, I felt the chill in my bones intensify. My right arm was completely numb now, from my fingertips to the base of my shoulder. In a small way, I was thankful. It meant I didn't need to feel the cuff as it squeezed the life out of me.

The demon kept pace beside me, eyes straight ahead and shoulders stiff. Every once in a while I'd sneak a peek at Jax and wonder what he was thinking in there. I couldn't imagine a guy like him being cooped up for so long.

"What happens if we don't make it?" I asked, a lump forming in my throat. We had less than twenty-four hours left to find a Fakori descendant or kill Malphi, both tall orders.

"We will make it."

"And if we don't? I'll die."

"No one will be able to claim you, if that's what weighs on your mind." The demon didn't break stride. "The theories are correct. Once you perished and were returned to your body, your power became unclaimable in death. You must give permission."

"But if this has never happened before, then how do we know for sure."

Jax's body stopped walking and turned to me. It was unsettling to see the soulless black orbs where his gray eyes should have been. "I know because I tried."

I balked. "You *tried*? As in, to claim me?"

"Of course," it said, as if I were stupid for even asking. With a quirk of an eyebrow and bemused tilt of Jax's lip, the demon started walking again.

I took a deep breath and followed after it. "But that's not what I meant, anyway. I'm talking about Jax."

"You're inquiring if I will relinquish control."

I nodded. It was all I could manage. The thought of dying before I'd even had much of a chance to actually live terrified me. But not as much as knowing Jax would be lost as well—that was, gone completely. If I died I knew he'd never be the same. If I were in his shoes, I would crumble. There wouldn't be a way to come back from that. But he was stronger than me. That fact was a small comfort as I faced the bleak circumstance ahead. The only thing left to hope was that the demon would give him back his body.

"If we fail and you die—" Jax's cell sounded, a heavy, grinding guitar solo from one of his favorite bands. Azirak fished the phone from his pocket and put it to Jax's ear. The call was short, and the demon said nothing to whoever was on the other end. When he hung up, he turned to me. "You will not die, Samantha Merrick. They have located the human, Fakori."

Chapter Nineteen

JAX/AZIRAK

The Fakori descendant wasn't far from Harlow. After Azi hung up with its informant, it dialed another clan member and told it where to pick us up. The car had just arrived, driven by a blond-haired female demon who looked extremely unhappy. It wasn't the only one.

"I can't believe I'm willingly getting into a car driven by a demon," Sam said as the vehicle pulled over to the side of the road. "Somewhere in hell, it's snowing."

"It does not snow in hell," Azi retorted.

Idiot. I gave a verbal sneer. *It's an expression.*

"I am aware," it responded. Stepping up to the car to open the door, the demon moved aside and gestured for Sam to get into the backseat.

She hesitated, probably wondering why the demon was talking to itself. "Huh?"

"Jax," it said. I felt the awkwardness as it said my name. "He finds me—"

"Annoying?" Sam supplied as Azi lowered my body into the passenger's seat. "Foul, manipulative, murderous?"

Azi laughed. "I imagine so." The car rolled back onto the road. "You forget that I did not ask for this. I am imprisoned here. Shackled to this plain, to this mortal, until he dies. And then, the cycle will begin again. My torture is unending."

"Torture which you deserve," she said, justified.

Anger flooded me, and I worried Sam would push the demon too far. My own rage was tenuous, balanced on the edge of a knife at any given moment. Azirak's was far more combustible. Easier to incite.

"It is my nature to conquer. To dominate. You know nothing of the war or the incident that caused it. We were justified in our attacks."

"To be honest, I couldn't care less. What matters to me is Jax and the affect you have on him. I know it's not your fault—that you had no choice. And from what I've seen, you're not the most horrible demon in the world. But you hurt him. Whether you mean to or not, you cause him pain."

"That is not my intention. I simply desire to exist." The demon cast a sidelong glance at the female driving the car. "And to see my clan flourish." It wasn't the truth, yet it wasn't a lie, either.

Sam must have taken the hint. With one of Azi's clan members in the car, bringing up the future, or its plans about what to do with her, was a bad idea. We needed their help.

We pulled up alongside the curb of a small yellow Cape Cod style cottage just after one in the afternoon. Chase put the cuff on Sam somewhere around midnight. That left eleven hours. If this went off without a hitch, then we were golden. Sam would be fine, and Malphi could live.

For now.

"This is it?" Sam whispered as she got out of the car. "This is where Fakori's descendant lives?"

Azirak nodded in confirmation, then turned to the female demon. "Wait for us here."

We made our way up the foliage-lined walk. When we reached the door, Sam went to knock, but it was already opened. A tendril of gray rose into the air as Azirak shouldered her aside and pushed into the house.

With each step my sense of dread grew. I wasn't alone. Azi was agitated, what I'd come to interpret as the demonic equivalent of worried. Through the living room and into the hall, there was nothing obviously out of place. No signs of struggle—until we reached the kitchen.

Sam let out an anguished howl and threw herself forward. She landed on her knees in a growing pool of blood beside an older man. "Do something," she screamed. She lifted the man's shoulders off the ground, pulling him up and cradling him close. "Don't let him die!"

The demon knelt across from her. I felt its remorse. "It is too late. The human is dead."

"Find another," Sam demanded. Tears streaked her face. "Get on the phone. Call your clan. Find another Fakori."

The demon shook my head. "There is no other. David Fakori was the last of his line."

Sam opened her mouth but no sound came. The tears began streaming freely down her cheeks and I lost it. Agreement forgotten, I pushed for control. I couldn't see her like that, on the verge of falling apart, and do nothing. She needed me.

The demon fought me at first, but it didn't last. Sam let out a wail and fell back against the counter, and Azirak moved aside. It hated that she was in pain, and knew I was the only one who'd be able to help.

"Sammy." I dove forward, my knee slipping in the blood,

and caught her before she toppled sideways. "Don't," I whispered, pulling her close. "We still have time."

"There's time," she agreed, between sobs. "But no options. This was my last feasible chance."

"No. Michael said—"

She pulled away and faced me, eyes cold and full of fury. "You had him killed," she spat.

"Sammy, what—" And then I understood. Azirak. She was talking to the demon. I shook my head and grabbed her hands. "It wasn't Azi. I'd know. It wasn't—"

"You never did like playing by the rules, brother." From the other end of the room, Chase walked into the kitchen. The front of his shirt and jeans were covered in blood. "I couldn't allow cheating."

Sam let out an agonized howl and launched herself upright. She dove for him, and, surprised, I wasn't able to grab in her time. "The world ends if Jax kills you," she screamed. "I'm free to do what I want."

Chase let her pin him against the counter. He even let her grab the butcher knife next to the sink and hold it to his throat. With an amused chuckle, he said, "Looks like the cuff is doing a number on you, Samantha." He pointed to the clock above the door. "Time's running out. You should focus on Malphi—something you should have done in the first place."

The knife broke through his skin as Sam shook with rage. Part of it was mine, feeding her actions through the link, but there was a portion of it that was all hers. After years of carrying a feeling of helplessness, reliving the night her parents were killed, she'd reached a breaking point. Pushed by the situation, or simply by the culmination of everything that had happened over the last few months, the seams of her control were ripping.

"Take it off," she growled.

Chase only laughed. "This side of you is damn sexy, Samantha, and while it's hard to resist you, I'm going to have to decline." In a swift movement he had their positions reversed, minus the knife. "But if you don't wish to eliminate Malphi, you can allow me to claim you and I'll remove the cuff."

I jumped to my feet and wrapped my fingers around a handful of his shirt. Hauling him back, I slammed him into the far wall.

He clucked his tongue, never losing his smile. "Don't do it. You might not care about the fate of the world, Jax, but you kill me and she's dead, too."

Azi raged inside me, flashing scene after scene — multiple, bloody ways to take Chase out. I felt the urge hum through every part of my body. It vibrated deep inside, waking something I kept buried deep. The borderline euphoric feeling that his death promised lingered just within my reach. All it would take was a single move. An instantaneous act that meant freedom from the pain and guilt I'd grown up with. Forget about Zenak. Screw Azirak. Chase might be my brother, but he was a bad person. And I fed on bad people, right? A part of me was terrified at the ease with which my mind justified it all. But it was more complicated than that.

If I killed him, Sam would die.

If I didn't kill him, Malphi would have to die.

"Jax!"

My grip loosened and I stepped away. Chase beamed, an expression full of smug satisfaction. He was untouchable and knew it. "That's better," he said, glancing up at the clock. "There's still time, Jax. You can still save her."

I backed away, feeling more helpless than I ever had. I would find Malphi. I would try to kill it. But I wouldn't succeed. I knew now that the hold Azirak had over me wasn't something I could compete with. I could fight the monster. Most of the time, I could win. But when it came to Malphi, I had no delusions. Azirak would not allow its mate to die.

"Sammy," I said. My throat felt thick. "Let's go."

Chapter Twenty

SAM

Jax took my hand and led me through the house. It was all a blur. I looked down at myself and saw that my jeans were stained with red. The blood of a stranger, someone like me, caught in the crossfire of a war we had no stake in. He'd been killed simply because the blood that flowed through him could have saved my life. He hadn't deserved this...

We emerged from the house to find the female demon still waiting. The last thing I wanted was to get in that car. I was out of options, hours away from dying. I didn't want to spend my remaining moments on Earth with a demon.

At least, not that demon.

When we reached the car, I stopped and turned to Jax. "I don't want to die." The words came out so low that I thought maybe he didn't hear me. "Please, don't let me go. I just— we—I'll do anything to stay."

The agony in his expression stole my breath. The corner of his eyes glistened as he sucked in a breath. He grabbed my face, fingers digging into the skin. "I'll kill the bitch, Sammy. I will."

It wasn't me he was trying to convince though. It was himself. I shook my head. "No, Jax. You won't."

I watched it happen. He shattered before me, throwing his head back and letting out a scream that could have chilled the arctic. The sound blasted right through me. I felt it from the tips of my toes to the bottom of every strand of hair. Balling his fist tight, Jax slammed it down against the roof of the car, caving the side in almost a foot. Our demonic chauffer said nothing.

I waited for his breathing to even out then gingerly took his hand. He was bleeding. The torn metal had sliced the pinkie side of his palm in an ugly gash. "I don't know much about being a Pure." My heart thundered inside my chest. The words came without thought. "I've seen what—what they can do. Demons. The ways they try to break you down to get what they want." The memory of what I'd watched them do to my mother when I was a child was permanently burned into my brain. "I can't—if they find me before I... Whoever gets to me will have the ability to lay claim. I don't know if I have the strength to hold out. You should do it first. Before it comes down to torture…"

His eyes widened. "What—"

"The angel said she would remove the cuff if I allowed her to claim me. That she *could* remove the cuff." I moved closer to him, taking comfort in his warmth. "You can get this thing off."

"If the situation is right." He repeated Michael's words. A small ember of hope burned inside me. But Jax didn't share my enthusiasm. He shook his head and took a step away from me. "Don't forget that if I do it, Azirak gains control over you. We don't know what will happen. You could—"

"Die?" I finished for him. "That's going to happen anyway.

At this point there's nothing to lose."

"Except giving a shitload of power to a demon."

It was my turn to take a step back. A sharp pain cut through me, and I found it hard to breathe. I forced the air into my lungs and cringed. "So you'd rather watch me die?"

His expression was stricken. Good. I knew exactly how he felt. He slammed his hand down again and the car groaned in protest. "Fuck! Sammy, I didn't mean—"

"For you to die would be a terrible waste," a new voice said.

We spun around. Standing on the pathway was a woman I'd never seen, with long, side swept brown hair and vibrant green eyes. She wasn't alone. With her, on either side, were two identical men, both total chrome domes, *a la* Mr. Clean, wearing white suits and sour expressions.

"And you are?" Jax asked, stepping between us.

"Her new master," the woman said.

"Like hell," he fired back. He turned to me and opened his mouth, but no sound came. He tried again, this time grabbing his throat and staggering back. It was like he couldn't breathe.

The woman turned to me and smiled. "Do you agree to be claimed?"

Jax's knees buckled as he fought for air. His eyes went wide, and his head shook vigorously. Seeing him like this, suffering, was enough to rip me wide open, but once I agreed, there was no coming back. Moments ago, allowing someone to claim me had seemed like my only option, but something told me these guys wouldn't play by the rules.

I squared my shoulders and stood my ground. "No."

The woman—angel or demon, I had no idea—didn't expect that answer. She faltered for a moment, surprised, but finally nodded. "I see," she said, placing an arm on the shoulder of both men beside her. "Then I suppose I will just need to convince you."

The two men came forward. I could have tried to run, but I knew it was pointless. Angel or demon, they would be on me faster than flies on shit. They grabbed me, and as Jax finally climbed to his feet, dragged me away.

My head hurt, a needle-like jabbing pricking my skull from the inside out. I opened my eyes, but there was only darkness. The air was musty. A basement or cave. There was mildew, too. I was allergic and my nose itched something fierce. My last few hours on Earth and I was going to spend them in an allergen induced haze.

I brought my hand up to scratch, but nothing happened. I was restrained. My hands and my feet. Huh. I'd only been tied up a couple of times before this. Both those activities had been more than fun. It was less interesting when done out of the bedroom.

I managed to wiggle my fingers, which was good since pins and needles had set in. I'd been out awhile. My legs were asleep and my neck ached.

Jax. He would have been fine after we left, right? Been able to breathe?

I flexed my foot and twisted my ankle. The ground was gravely, like loose rock and pebble or something. I could have tried calling out, but the chances of someone other than one of my captors being within hearing distance was probably one in a billion.

Tugging and twisting, I yanked hard on my restraints. Whatever they were made of, they were smooth and cold—not metal, but just as strong. Breaking them wasn't an option.

"While it amuses me to watch you struggle, it wastes time," a woman's voice said from the darkness.

Light flooded the room, and when my eyes finally

adjusted, she was settling in a chair a few feet in front of me. I'd been right. We were in some kind of basement. Boxes covered in dust, shelves with old books, nothing special or out of the ordinary. Nothing useful.

"The house belonged to the Kendal family," she said, tapping her head. "I can hear your thoughts." She frowned, watching me intently. After a few moments, she sighed. "Yes. They're dead. Regrettably it was our only choice."

"Of course it was," I said drily.

She leaned forward, elbows balanced on her knees. "Do you agree to be claimed?"

I stared at her. "Seriously? Why would my answer have changed between now and the last time you asked?"

She sighed. "Do you know what you are?"

"Yes."

"Do you know what hell could do with you? The damage and pain they could inflict?"

"Oh," I said, flashing her a concerned frown. "I get it now. You're worried about humanity. Is that right?"

She looked insulted. "I am a child of God."

Well, that answered the angel or demon question. "If you're an angel, where are your wings?"

A burst of wind rolled over me, and with a loud whooshing, the angel's wings unfurled. Beautifully colored, in vivid hues of blue and green, they filled half the room.

"How come they're blue?" Truthfully, I didn't give a crap about the color. They could have been neon tie-dye with rainbow colored cows. But keeping up the conversation might stall whatever she had planned.

"The color is representative of my rank."

"Rank, huh?" I swallowed the bile creeping up my throat. "So blue stands for, what? Kitchen staff?"

She didn't answer.

"Oh. I know. You're heaven's Chief toilet scrubber?"

"I am a general in the Army of Heaven" She said tightly. "Enough of this banter. You will consent to be claimed. I will leave you no other choice."

"That sounds like a threat," I said, doing my best to keep my voice from wobbling.

"Merely a fact."

"So the torture thing. That stands, huh?"

The angel stood and took two steps forward until she was towering over me. "We will do what's necessary."

I swallowed back a lump of fear. Jax would find me. I had complete confidence. The question was, would he find me before or after this woman made mush of my brains?

"So…that's a yes on the torture, then?"

Chapter Twenty-One

JAX

As soon as I was able to stand, I pulled open the car door. The female demon behind the wheel stared straight ahead, her eyes glazed and unseeing. At her throat, a wicked gash still oozed blood. I unfastened her seat belt and jerked her from the seat, then slid behind the wheel and cranked the engine.

I drove until I couldn't stand it anymore. Azi, like me, was worried about Sam. Whether it was because of its feelings for her, or because it was worried she'd be claimed by someone else, I didn't know and didn't care. Right now, we had a common goal—just as soon as I calmed the thing down. Rage seeped into the air all around me, and eventually I had to pull the car over just to keep from ripping off the steering wheel. I was driving in circles with no clue where the fuck to go, or what the hell to do next.

Feed. The single word nearly shattered my skull.

Just seven hours on the clock. I didn't want to waste time,

but I felt the need as strongly as the demon did. Just as it fed off the pain and anger of others, I'd come to realize, I did the same. Not in exactly the same way, but the demon's moods influenced me more now that I'd embraced it. Its weakness was mine.

I pulled into a Quick Stop parking lot, and the moment I stepped from the car, I smelled it. Fear. It was easy to track, around the side of the building to a single car parked at the far end of the row. I crept along the shadows, waiting. Watching.

The man in the driver's seat was screaming at a small boy. He grabbed the kid by the hair, shaking him roughly before leaning across and opening the door to shove him out. The child had to go to the bathroom. The bastard didn't like stopping. He was going to miss the start of his favorite television show.

The kid closed the door and scurried around the building, presumably to get the restroom key from the clerk inside. Azi shuddered in anticipation. I did, too. My feet carried me from the shadows, across the lot, and to the man's car. He was looking down at his cell phone so he didn't see me approach. It made yanking the door open and dragging him out that much sweeter.

"What the —"

I shoved him up against the hood. My fingers dug into skin, through the thin material of his shirt. The sensation sent a ripple of contentment through me. "You think hitting a kid makes you a big man?"

His breath reeked of alcohol and his colors swirled crimson. No fear. Anger. He was pissed I'd had the nerve to step in.

This was just what I needed. Moments like these made me sick. I *wanted* to give in. Craved the feeling that came over me when the demon fed. It was a high like no other, filling me with an unparalleled sense of exhilaration.

He pushed off the car and swung out hard, but I stepped

to the side, missing the blow easily, and followed through with one of my own. A kidney shot, it landed with precision, and Azi went wild, greedily sucking down the man's rage.

He recovered, stumbling a little, and tried again. This time he rushed me, intent on grinding me into the brick wall at my back. I pivoted and changed position, and he flew right past, crashing into the wall instead of me.

I grabbed a handful of his hair, like he'd done with the kid, and shoved his face hard into the bricks. "Touch him again and I'll kill you. We clear?"

The man didn't answer. Instead, he struggled against my grip, still trying to free himself and get in a good shot. More. Azi wanted more. It wanted pain. So that's what I gave it. I pushed, dragging the side of his face along the wall for about a foot. He screamed, leaving a trail of skin and blood where the stone grated him. "Asking again—we clear?"

"Dad?"

I spun to see the kid standing by the car with a look of horror on his face.

"Go get the cops, Kenny," the man sputtered. He still struggled, but more weakly. He knew he was beat.

I let go of him and stepped away. With a nod to the kid, I said, "No need to do that, Kenny. Your dad and I were just having a chat about how he treats you." I turned back to the guy. "That right?"

The man narrowed his eyes but said nothing.

"He's gonna be nicer from now on," I said, walking back toward my car.

Though not as potent as a demon kill, the violence settled Azi enough for me to focus. Sam and I were linked. That had to mean I could find her. I just had to try.

Once I was back in the car, I took a deep breath and closed my eyes. Azi flashed an image of her face and my heartbeat went into overdrive. In the vision, she was bruised and bleeding, with a busted lip and a wide gash on her right cheek.

"No," I snapped, shaking the likeness from my mind. "She's okay. I would know if she wasn't."

The demon wasn't convinced, but it settled down to let me concentrate. I'd never tried using the link between us. Up until now, it'd been more of a hassle than anything else, making me hyperaware of every detail about Sam. Her moods and emotions. Her body… I'd hated it because it rubbed my nose in the one thing I wanted but couldn't have. Now I had to rely on it. Talk about fucked up.

I sat behind the wheel with my eyes closed. It took a while, but I finally felt her. Felt her fear. It was just as potent as if she were sitting beside me. She was someplace dark. And cold. But other than that, I had no clue.

"Shit!" I slammed my hand against the dash, leaving a fist sized indentation. I had no way of finding her. There wouldn't be a ransom. No one would call for a trade. They had exactly what they wanted. They held all the fucking cards.

Azi sent more images of her, a dizzying mix of jumbled moments from over the years.

I gripped the wheel hard and closed my eyes to stop the spinning. "How," I growled. "How the fuck am I supposed to find her?"

Another rush of pictures came, so strong I almost puked. They went too fast to make out much detail, but I did notice a common thread. Azirak's demons.

"They won't help me," I said, twisting the ignition key a little too hard. "I screwed them over by letting Chase walk away. Cheated them out of their power."

Azi wasn't deterred, and they kept coming. Sam. Azirak's demons. Sam. Demons. The wheels in my head started turning. We had several common enemies in Zenak, his clan, and the angels. If I sought them out and said I wanted to gain a Pure with the intention of hunting down Zenak, they might be forgiving. They were desperate to regain their power. A few hours ago it'd been Azirak in control of my body. He'd called his clan to locate the Fakori descendant. All I had to do was keep them thinking the demon still had the wheel. The only bump in the road would be Malphi.

As if in response, Azi communicated a scene of me embracing the dark, faceless female, and then another, of Sam wrapped tightly in my arms. The feeling that came with both was the same. Need. Desire. Longing. Getting close to Malphi was risky, but I had no other choice. I had no intention of losing Sam again.

"How do I find them?"

A single picture. The Inferno.

G etting back to Harlow took forever. At least, that's how it felt. Each second was one I wasn't trying to find Sam. Every minute was one that they might hurt her. If anything happened, I would bring hell to their doorstep in ways they couldn't possibly imagine.

It was almost three by the time I pulled up in front of the bar. The place was fairly empty, as usual, and the bartender—a demon I'd never seen before—gave a slight nod as I walked in.

"Heckle here?"

The bartender shook his head. "Nope." He looked me up and down. "*Out of town.*"

I didn't give a shit what the euphemism was for. I only wanted information. "I'm looking for one of Azirak's clan."

"Never heard of 'em," he replied, and nodded to the liquor shelves. "What d'ya want?"

I leaned forward and inhaled. The bartender wasn't

Zenak's. Not Azirak's. Definitely a demon, though.

Factionless. I had no idea where the word came from, but knew without a doubt I was right. This demon was neither mine nor Chase's.

I reached across the bar and grabbed its shirt, yanking forward. The demon dropped the bottle in its hand, the glass shattering against the edge of the counter and dumping vodka all over the floor. "I'll say it louder, just in case you didn't hear me the first time. I'm looking for one of Azirak's clan."

It wasn't until the demon looked at me — more specifically, my eyes — that he realized who I was. His head dipped and he opened his mouth, but someone else spoke for him.

"I am of Azirak's — "

I turned to face it.

Tall, with dirty blond hair and narrow shoulders, the newcomer curled its lip back and tensed, ready for a fight. "You!"

Time to put my game face on. I had to sell this shit good. "I have control of the body," I said with a subtle nod. I let go of the bartender and leaned back against the bar.

It wasn't a demon I recognized, but obviously it recognized me. "You betrayed us!"

"The human betrayed you," I corrected, hoping Azi went along with the charade. "Who's your leader?"

"You are," it said angrily. The demon's eyes narrowed as it regarded me with caution.

"I've been otherwise engaged. Who was in charge in my absence?"

"Ranook," it said, almost hesitantly. I'd expected the answer to be Malphi. "Why?"

"Take me to Ranook."

It blinked, staring at me for several more seconds. "Why would I do that?"

I offered it a wicked grin. "Because I've got information that will change everything."

Chapter Twenty-Two

SAM

She'd been sitting across from me, just staring, for almost twenty minutes now. Normally I could pull a stare down with the best of them, but something about the angel's eyes creeped me the hell out. "Are we going to do this all day?" I asked. "Gaze into each other's eyes? Because I'll be honest with you…you're not my type."

"Ahh, yes," she responded with a grimace. "Your type is a bit darker, isn't it?"

I shrugged. "All girls love the bad boys."

"And I wasn't gazing into your eyes. I was gazing into your head."

"My head?" Not exactly something I wanted to hear.

She stood and came closer, head cocked to the side. "Trying to see your fears. The things you hold dear. But, I'm getting ahead of myself. I've been rude and I apologize. I never introduced myself. My name is Anella."

"Well, Anella, I'm Sam, and I'd like to go home."

"You are brave for a human." She laughed, and I tried not to take it personally. "Or foolish. It's so hard to tell with your kind."

I shrugged, doing my best not to cringe when the bindings on my hands pulled tighter. "What can I say? Probably a little bit of both."

"Agree to be claimed," she said, bending down so that we were eye to eye.

"Let me go and I'll think about it?" It was worth a shot, at least.

Anella sighed. I had a feeling I was grating on her patience. She placed a hand on either side of my neck. I could feel her touch through my clothing. In fact, it was really warm. Hot.

Scorching.

"What—? Oh my God." I gasped. The pain increased until I was nearly blinded by it. There was a smell in the air. Singed hair and what I guessed was my burning flesh. I tried to hold back, but it was impossible. A deafening scream spilled from my lips.

The music was loud. I felt it thumping in my bones. A steady, hypnotic rhythm that made me want to move my body. Or, maybe it was Jax, pressed close behind me and swaying his hips in a way that made my mind wander to dark, forbidden things.

We were in the middle of the dance floor at the Viking. Alone. A nagging voice whispered in my ear that this wasn't right. We shouldn't be here. Not like this. But as the beat intensified and the lights dimmed, I let it go. All that mattered was now. This electric, alive feeling.

"I love the way you move," Jax whispered in my ear. The sound of his voice, oddly clear over the rumbling beat, was like a flamethrower to my skin. His tongue flicked out, skimming the edge of my earlobe just a second before he nipped it.

He draped his arms around my shoulders from behind, hands pressing flat against my chest. Slowly, still moving his hips to the music, he slid his hands downward, between my breasts. I gasped as he paused just beneath them, then jerked his hands up to cup each one. His warmth bled through the thin material of my shirt. I covered his hands with mine and pushed back, grinding myself into him.

He chuckled. Leaning forward, he said at my ear, "I know what you want." With his thumb and pointer, he squeezed the right nipple and twisted—just a little—and I inhaled sharply. He laughed again and continued to slide his hands down until he came to the waist of my jeans. Playing with the button, he said, "Is this it?"

I bit my lip.

He slipped the button through the hole and slid the zipper down an inch, letting his thumb slip behind the fabric. Sliding it back and forth, frustratingly slow, he added, "Or, is this it?"

Every inch of me was ready to combust. My pulse was off the charts and my heart was about to break free of my chest.

He laughed again, a dark chime that made the hairs on the back of my neck and arms jump to attention. Pushing his finger a little further, he pressed it into me, stopping just shy of slipping inside. "I'll do it," Jax said. "I'll make you scream. Right here. Right now. You just have to do one thing for me."

God. Anything. I would do anything. It was taking all my self-control not to push his hand where I desperately wanted it to be.

He laughed. He had me wrapped around his little finger and he knew it. Then again, Jax had control over me. My body, my heart and soul. Everything that was me belonged to him. "Let me claim you."

I froze. The music stopped, and my heart, so close to

imploding, seemed to stutter and come to a frightening standstill.

"Come on, Sammy. All I'm asking is that you be mine. Let me claim you." He pulled my hair back with his free hand and nibbled on the tip of my ear. "Agree and I'll show you things you never dreamed of."

I shook my head and closed my eyes tight. It's what I wanted. A few hours ago, I'd practically begged him to do it to save my life. For some reason, though, now it seemed like a bad idea. Something had changed, and even though I couldn't quite put my finger on it, I knew deep in my gut that it was a bad idea. "No. I can't—"

"Fine," he snapped. I opened my eyes to find him across the room, on a couch that hadn't been there before. He wasn't alone.

The girl beneath him sighed loudly, turning her head. Our eyes met, and Sadie grinned at me from behind long, thick lashes. "Baby," she cooed, keeping her eyes on mine. "*I'll* let you claim me anytime."

Jax chuckled and looked up, and all the air rushed from my lungs. "She's willing to let me do whatever I want…" He bent his head and took a chunk of the skin on her neck between his teeth. Horrified, I watched as he bit down and pulled, tearing the flesh.

Sadie laughed and arched her back as the blood flowed freely from her wounds. "Oh, baby. You know just how I like it."

Wrong. This was wrong in so many ways. Little things began to creep up on me. The club, previously spotless and empty, had a dilapidated look. Around the edge of the dance floor there were boxes piled halfway to the ceiling, stacked next to shelving units and old lawn equipment. The pristine tile beneath our feet dulled and lost its color, springing spider web cracks in places I knew there were none.

Jax stood, shoving Sadie away from him, and made his way back to me. "Say the word," he whispered against my ear. "Allow me to claim you, and I'll get rid of the witch." He pressed himself close, but something was different now. He'd lost his warmth. Instead of the inferno he'd been only moments ago, all passionate and wanting, his body felt cold. Dead, almost. One hand wrapped around my waist, forearm grazing bare skin, while the other wrapped loosely around my neck from behind.

I tried to pull away, but he held brutally tight. Panic rose in my throat, and I screamed as the rest of the illusion peeled away to reveal the basement. I was shoved forward and I stumbled, landing hard on my knees across the room.

"Bitch," the angel spat. She sighed and nodded toward the stairs. There was a shadow standing at the top. "Time for plan B."

Chapter Twenty-Three

Ranook lived on the outskirts of Harlow, a few blocks from the police station. Tazari, the demon I'd found at the Inferno, called to say we were on our way. I'd overheard the conversation. While Tazari wasn't enthused, Ranook sounded excited. The return of the prodigal leader was something they'd been working toward.

The apartment building was one of the better ones in this part of town. Working elevator and functioning locks on the entry door—it was heaven compared to some of the shit holes I'd stayed in over the years. But when you had a tendency toward violence, things had a way of getting done. And from the smell, the entire building was inhabited by demons.

There were no humans in this place. Like the Inferno, it was strictly a demonic destination. That was fine. Less collateral damage should something go wrong. I felt zero guilt taking down a demon to feed. The way I saw it, dealing with them was a public service. One I was more than willing to provide.

"This way," Tazari said, leading me toward the elevator.

I grabbed its arm as it pushed the up button. "No." I could take the demon down with both hands tied behind my back, but that didn't mean I wanted to be trapped in a steel cage with it. For all I knew, there were a half dozen others waiting to ambush me. I nodded to the stairs. "We will take the stairs." I almost added you dirty fucker but caught myself at the last minute. They had to believe I was Azirak.

If Tazari was pissed, it didn't show. With a curt nod the demon climbed the stairs, annoyingly slow, as I followed behind until we reached Ranook's apartment on the fourth floor.

"Fair warning," I said as it raised its hand to knock. "I will rip you apart if this is a trick."

The demon bowed its head. "No trick, my lord. But be warned. Not all our faction will be pleased to see you after…"

"After the human let Zenak go free?" I finished.

He nodded. "Yes."

"And you? How do you feel about me?"

The demon shifted from foot to foot, nervous. It didn't answer.

"I take it you're not thrilled to see me, then?" As I spoke, Azirak rumbled, angry. It bled into the air around me, pulling at the edge of my control. My limbs were moving before I gave it much thought. I grabbed the demon around the neck and slammed it up against the door. "I am your leader." The words came from Azi, but also from me. My demon felt betrayed by this minion's lack of respect, and I, in turn, felt it as well. "Your general. You dare show me disrespect?"

The demon's eyes widened, like it was seeing me for the first time. I'd have to try harder. Obviously I hadn't been selling *demonic overlord* hard enough. It sputtered, hands coming up to loosen my grip.

I pulled back and slammed it against the door again. "Do not test me, Tazari. I think you'll find me far less merciful than I used to be."

The door opened and I let the demon fall back into the apartment. It hit the floor then stumbled up and away, as far out of my reach as it could go. Azi was satisfied by this. I liked it, too. The feeling of power was heady, and as I leveled my gaze at it, I swear the lesser demon trembled in fear.

"Azirak," a tall demon said, stepping up to the door. It held out its hand. "I am Ranook."

The instinct was to take its hand, but Azi didn't want me to. Ranook was no friend. "I know who you are."

"Forgive me." It withdrew the hand, unaffected by the slight. "Tazari says you are looking for me. What can I do for you?"

The question pissed Azi off. A flash bombarded my mind. Two large figures, inhuman and distorted, on a battlefield. They faced off each other as war raged all around them. Azirak and Ranook. A rush of memory and I knew the demon had challenged mine for leadership once. The coup had failed, but things were never the same. Azi didn't trust his clan mate.

"I see you've taken advantage of my absence," I said.

Ranook bowed its head. "Forgive me, my lord. Someone needed to guide them while you were…away." It looked up and there was a gleam of defiance in its eyes. "Have you beaten down the human at last? Returned to us?"

"I was never gone," I growled, partially for show, and partially because Azi was fuming.

"You let Zenak escape," Ranook said with a fake smile. "You forfeited our birth right to save your human's brother."

"Letting Zenak go was not to save—" I almost said Chase but stopped just in time. "The human. It was because something much more important was brought to my attention."

"Oh?" Ranook said, "What could be more important

than gaining back our power?"

"Gaining more power."

"More power?" The other demon laughed. "And what source did you happen upon that warranted betraying your clan?"

I lunged forward and grabbed the front of his shirt, dragging him several inches off the ground. "A Pure."

"A Pure? Impossible!"

"The girl. Samantha Merrick. She's a Pure."

"How can you know that? She—"

"With her power, I have no need to spill Zenak's blood. I will use her to destroy the entire clan."

Ranook stared in disbelief. "I don't believe it."

I drew myself up. "You dare question me?"

"How," it said with a bit more challenge. "How is it the girl is a Pure yet still alive?"

"Her heart stopped and the power was activated," I said. "And I will claim it."

I wasn't sure whose words were spilling from my lips. Mine, or Azirak's.

Chapter Twenty-Four

SAM

"You know that I thought about you, right?" Jax said. He was on the ground, leaning back against a large pine tree, and I was wedged between his legs, leaning against his chest. "Every day that I was gone."

"Yeah," I answered. "I thought about you, too."

The sun was going down, and the clouds had taken on a pinkish-orange hue. This was nice. Perfect, even. Being here with Jax, doing something normal couples did, was like heaven. I'd earned a little heaven.

Jax played with a strand of my hair, winding it around his pointer finger. "Rick asked us to come for dinner tonight. Up for it?"

The answer lodged in my throat. Dinner at Rick's was always a plus. He could cook like no one else I knew. But the invitation felt wrong. An uneasy feeling wormed its way into my stomach, but I pushed it off.

"Sure. Sounds like a plan." I took a deep breath. "Do you

ever wonder what would have happened if you'd told me the truth that night? About the demon?"

He let go of my hair and wrapped both arms around me. "I thought about it. A lot."

"How come you never did it? I mean, you had to know it wouldn't change things. Right?"

"In my gut, yeah. But on the surface? I think other than hurting you, Chase, or Rick, that was my biggest fear—that I'd have the balls to tell you, and you'd turn away."

I twisted around and sat up on my knees facing him. "I'd never turn away. I've seen the ugliest parts of you, Jax Flynn. The darkest and the most violent. But I've also seen the most amazing brightness. Pure light and love and compassion that should be impossible after going through what you have."

He cupped the sides of my face and leaned in, kissing me gently on the forehead, then again on the lips. It was the softest brush. Tentative and sweet. He climbed to his feet and held out a hand to me. "You are a miracle."

I took it and smiled. "Miracle enough to get a milkshake on the way to Rick's?"

"Anything you want, Sammy." He leaned in to kiss me again, but froze halfway there. I gasped. Someone was standing behind him.

I opened my mouth to scream. To tell him to move away, but it was too late. A dark stain appeared and began to spread across his chest. At first it looked black, like someone had spilled a perfect inky circle in the middle of his shirt. But as it grew, it became obvious that it was red.

The figure behind him stepped into the fading light and draped both arms around Jax's shoulders. "Fancy meetin' you here," Chase said with a laugh, then jammed something hard, forward. The tip of an object, something sharp, broke through with the sound of cracking bone, and protruded from the center of the stain on Jax's chest.

Jax was horrified. He blinked twice, then brought a finger to the blood, swiping it across and lifting his hand to see it. "Sammy—"

I grabbed him and we fell to the ground together. "No," I repeated. Over and over, I said it, as though it would change things. Undo what had been done.

Jax coughed and blood trickled from the corner of his mouth. A thin line, so much like the time he'd bitten the corner of his lip while trying to steal my cotton candy at the county fair. "I—"

"Shh," I said, pressing a finger to his lips. Lips that already felt so cold. That was impossible, right? He couldn't be this cold. Not…no.

"Time is short, Samantha," Chase said. He grabbed me by the hair and dragged me to my feet. "I can save him if you let me."

"Yes," I screamed, yanking free from his grip. "Save him. I'll do anything."

He smiled, a triumphant grin that made me want to beat him till he bled. "Let me claim you. Let me claim you, and Jax will be safe. He'll be alive and free."

"No," I said, backing away one step at a time until I couldn't go any farther. The woods faded, and I was back in the basement, the mold and mildew scented air permeating my nose. The angel that'd been holding me the last time was a few feet away, the expression on her face murderous.

"Unless you consent," she said, slowly ascending the stairs. "You will watch him die a thousand times. And then, when you think you can no longer take it, we will kill him again. For real."

The door slammed and I was alone.

Chapter Twenty-Five

JAX

"It is good to have you back within the fold, my lord," Hileeka, a male demon said. It was sitting across from me, staring. What I wanted more than anything was to hit it. To make it bleed.

Unfortunately that wouldn't do much in the way of convincing them I was on their side.

As powerful as Azi was, I knew I had no hope of finding Sam on my own. I needed their resources. And to get their help, they needed to think their leader had returned. Azi wasn't happy about deceiving them. Every once in a while I felt the demon's anger at what I was doing, but it was overshadowed by concern for Sam. If this hadn't been about her, I doubted the demon would allow me to act out the ruse.

"So tell us," Ranook said, sitting next to Hileeka. "Where is the Pure now?"

"Angels have her." I knew it would get a reaction. I was right.

Ranook jumped from the couch and began pacing, spewing curses in a language that, while vaguely familiar, I didn't quite understand. Hileeka yelled something, and two other demons, a male and female, came running from the other room.

"This needs to be rectified," Ranook said, slamming a fist against the wall. "If they claim her—"

"They won't." I stood. This is where things could get tricky. The whole plan could explode. "Gather as many as you can and canvas the area. Do whatever it takes to find where they're keeping her."

"Yes, my lord."

Ranook stayed behind as the others went in search of information about Sam. Azi used the opportunity to set the record straight.

"I remember what you did the last time we met, Ranook," I found myself saying. Azi shimmied inside me, angry but excited. It flashed a series of pictures depicting the other demon's betrayal. "I remember all of it."

"As you should, my lord," it said in a deceptively calm voice. But it wasn't calm. Something stirred in my gut, and Azi pushed harder for the surface, gaining a bit of control, chasing the spark of fear that wafted from Ranook. "A good leader knows the battlefield. It knows its enemies."

I was on my feet, striding across the room. I grabbed a handful of the traitor's shirt and hefted upward. "You have twenty seconds to tell me why I shouldn't rip the head from your pathetic human body."

"Lord Azirak, what—"

The potent stench of its fear was addictive, sending wave after wave of contentment through me. In that moment, I wasn't me. I wasn't Azirak. We weren't a *we*. We were an *I*. "Ten seconds left."

Ranook tried in vain to free itself. It struggled frantically, but my grip was ironclad. "I—I know where she is," it said just as the fingers of my other hand slipped around its neck and began to squeeze. The idea of feeding off his dying breath became an obsession. "I can take you to her."

My fingers froze. "To Sam?" I set him down and stepped away. My heart began to race. Every nerve ending was alive and itching for...for what?

Ranook laughed, a dark chuckle tainted by anger. "To your betrothed. You can finally consummate your union. Make us stronger. Undefeatable." It's eyes lit with glee. "I can take you to everything you've been searching for. I can take you to Malphi."

R anook took me across the town line, just to the other side of Burke, and made me wait inside the car. Suspicious, I'd wanted to refuse, but Azi spoke for me, agreeing with an eerie enthusiasm. It'd been ten minutes now, and I was starting to get pissed.

"Don't get any ideas," I said to Azi out loud. "We're here to find Sam. Not provide you with a demonic hookup."

The demon's hesitation was easy to sense, but in the end it sent an image of Sam's face through my head as Ranook returned to the car. It wanted to find her as much as I did. "Malphi is looking forward to seeing you," Ranook said, opening my door. "Just as soon as you prove yourself..."

"Prove myself?" I slid from the car, tightening my fists against the urge to pummel them against the demon's face. Azi communicated another image, this one of my hands around Ranook's neck. I felt its skin beneath my fingers, the bones giving under the pressure. Its eyes bulged and it tried to speak. I squeezed harder. The scene ended, leaving me raw. If it didn't have something I needed, I would end the demon right now, taking immense pleasure in feeding from every last ounce of pain and fear as its essence faded. "You dare question my motives."

"If you would follow me, I will explain."

I slammed the door closed and followed Ranook up a long, twisting path toward an expansive Victorian house. A large porch, decorated in wicker furniture, wrapped around the impeccably kept home. Innocent. Peaceful, even. But one deep breath told me it was anything but. This was no human domicile. It was inhabited by demons.

Ranook pushed through the door with me on its heels. The inside of the house was like the outside. Innocuous and unassuming. A familiar scent hung in the air, but as hard as I tried, I couldn't place it. "Where is Malphi?"

"I told you," Ranook said. "You'll need to prove yourself. Malphi has been in hiding for safety reasons. Most of the others don't know that she's here."

What little patience I had was waning. "You're telling me Malphi is afraid of our clan?"

"Most of our clan is…angry with your mate. They distrust her motives." An image flashed through my mind. It was shadowed and impossible to make out the details, but I felt the emotion behind it—an overwhelming sense of anger and betrayal. "And it's no secret that Zenak wants her dead. She's been a constant threat to him in every one of her human incarnations." The demon chuckled. "She's killed him several times, you know. They have something of a history…"

"What do you mean, a history?"

"Your full memory will come back in time. With each human life you inhabit, it always does, but maybe this will help you." Ranook gestured to the floral disaster of a couch in the center of the room. "Malphi was presented to Zenak, chosen to be his mate by the Lord Lucifer. Unfortunately, she had already set her sights on you."

I sat, and the demon took the chair across from me. "Continue," I said.

"Before our exile, before the great war, you instructed her to go to him under the guise of acceptance. She was to kill him before their union was consummated and return to you."

"And did she?" I almost said it, but caught myself in time.

Ranook shrugged. A sly smile tugged at the corners of its lips. "She tried, but failed. Their union was consummated—by consent or force, it is unclear. You didn't care though. You wanted her back and so you took her."

"I stole her from Zenak."

The demon leaned back, kicking its feet onto the table. "I suppose you could say that Malphi is hell's own Helen of Troy."

"That's what started the war between our clans?"

"In part, yes. The two clans were always at odds, but not until Malphi was there such violence. It took the equivalent of two hundred Earth years to reacquire your love. During that time, Zenak was not…kind to her, fostering her hatred for him. Several times, after being born back to Earth, she has sought him out and ended his life before consummating her union with you. Unconsummated, Malphi was not a royal—"

"And by spilling Zenak's blood, was unable to end the exile," I finished, understanding. Azi stirred, furious at the memory, yet the affection it felt for Malphi was palatable. The potency of the feelings should have scared me. I needed to kill the demoness to save Sam, yet I found comfort in the affection. Familiarity and warmth.

"Yes," Ranook said. "You were understandably upset by her actions. Unlike this incarnation, your only goal was to restore your clan to its former glory. She made it impossible, and so you had to wait. Then when you were reborn, you and our enemy ended up in the body of twins…"

"Do not question my intentions," I warned, unnerved by the ferocity of my voice. It was Azi, and yet it was me as well. I was furious that he hinted at disloyalty. "I will see us restored, kings among sheep, as it should be." The words were meant to placate Ranook, a string of lies with only one intention. Saving Sam. Yet something about them rang with truth. "Get on with it. What does Malphi need me to do to prove myself?"

Ranook's grin widened. "In time, my lord. In time."

Chapter Twenty-Six

They'd finally given it a rest and gone back upstairs, but not without promising to return. Next time, the angel said before closing the door at the top of the stairs, they were going to start removing limbs. It wasn't my body they needed intact.

That was kind of hard to ignore.

A tremor rippled through me, and I bit back a sob. Crying wouldn't do any good, yet the tears welled up, slipping down my cheeks and leaving molten trails of desperation.

I closed my eyes and pictured Jax's face—sharp lines and stormy gray eyes that held the promise of danger, and just the smallest hint of vulnerability. Eyes I wanted desperately to see again.

My entire body ached, a throbbing pain that had nothing to do with the angel's attempt at getting me to consent. The demon cuff squeezed against my skin, sending a painful reminder of the ticking clock. With each hour, the frequency with which it contracted increased, and it made me wonder how bad it would get before it all ended. Would the pain be debilitating? Would I beg for death? Being confined to an obscure basement, stuck with the angels, didn't leave much wiggle room. But maybe this was better. Jax might want to kill Malphi to satisfy Chase's bargain, but Azi would never let him.

I bit back a gasp as another wave of pain came. The hinges of the door at the top of the stairs groaned open, letting a beam of light wash over the steps. A moment later, the wooden steps groaned beneath someone's weight.

"Have you come to your senses?" the female angel who'd brought me here asked. She was with another, a new male. He was over six feet tall, with broad shoulders and a cruel grin. "We have no wish to cause you pain, Samantha. If you do not allow me to claim you, the demon cuff will end your life. What a waste that will be."

"Then let me go," I tried. "Give me a fighting chance to get this thing off."

She frowned. It almost looked genuine. "If I could, I most certainly would. But to allow hell to obtain you would be devastating."

"Then we're all in luck," I said as another ripple of pain radiated. "That won't happen. I have no intention of letting myself be used for evil." I fixed my gaze on her. "Or your so-called good."

She sighed and shook her head, stepping to the side. The grim set of her lips screamed of irritation, but worse than that, determination. "I've tried to persuade you with methods that, while mentally disturbing, did not cause you any real harm. I'm afraid you leave me no choice."

The male angel stepped forward, towering over me. I didn't like the look in his eyes. Part excitement and part anger—equally dangerous. His movements were too quick to follow. His hand whipped around, a blur of motion followed by a world-rocking blow. My head snapped sideways, the room exploding until all that remained was a collection of shapeless, colored blobs and distorted sound.

When my vision cleared, I stretched my jaw, cringing when it went *snap-crackle-pop*. I'd been a trouble maker as a kid. Jax and I had gotten into more tight spots than I cared to admit, but I'd never been in a fight. I'd never taken an actual blow.

I tasted fresh blood, the metallic tang of it turning my stomach. The angel lifted a finger, rubbing it across my bottom lip, then lifting it to his own. "Consent to be claimed."

I spat out a mouthful of blood, making sure to get his shoes, and said, "Nope."

It was exactly what he wanted to hear. The spark of excitement in his eyes bloomed into an all-out four-alarm fire. He reached for me, hand curling into the material of my shirt, and hefted me off the seat. "Do you think this a game, human?"

"What I think," I said with as much courage as I could muster, "is that you're full of shit. You need my consent to get my power—which I'm not giving. You can try to scare me into it, but it's bullshit. If you were willing to kill me, you'd have done it already."

"You're correct. To waste your full potential would be criminal. I have no intention of killing you. But there are so many things on this earth that are far worse than death." He laughed and leaned in close. "Trust me. You *will* consent."

It was his voice, much more than the threat itself, that chilled me from the inside out. It held the promise of agony.

He lifted me higher, lips curving upward. "I believe it's time—"

"Mishca! Falel! Get—" The sentence cut off, followed by the sounds of chaos. A continuous stream of breaking glass and muffled screams sounded from the floor above us until it finally reached the door.

Four sets of feet slowly descended the stairs, in no particular hurry. Falel set me down, but didn't let go, and Mishca hissed at the newcomers. "Unclean," she spat. "You dare trespass on our ground?"

"You have something that belongs to us," one of the party crashers said. I tilted my head to the right, trying to ignore the not-so-subtle swimming in my brain at the movement, and saw the newcomers were demons.

"You will not take the Pure. I will spare your life if you leave now."

The quintet of demons laughed in unison. The tallest of them stepped to the front, hands on his hips and eyes fixed on me. "How about this: if *you* hand over the Pure, we will spare *your* lives."

"I've got a third option," I interjected as all heads swiveled in my direction. "Let me go, and I'll spare *all* your lives."

The demons thought it was hysterical—which I tried not to take personally—while the two angels remained deadpan. Mishca grabbed my wrist and wrenched me from Falel. "Come closer and we will kill her."

I tensed as she pulled out a wicked looking blade. The handle glowed an eerie purple and gave off a vibration I felt from head to toe. She jerked me sideways, wrapping an arm under my chin, and rested the blade against my throat. All the air left the room. The blade was warmer than you'd expect metal to be, like it'd been sitting next to a toasty fire—not that it made me feel better. I had no desire to have my throat slit by metal of any temperature.

The tall demon in front chuckled. If he was concerned, it didn't show. "You will not kill the Pure. You desire her power as much as we do. And we both know you can't have it unless she gives it to you willingly. To do that, she must be alive."

Falel stepped in front of us, pulling out his own freaky purple pig sticker. "If it means keeping it from you, we will gladly sacrifice her energy."

The demon shrugged and took a step back, folding his arms and flashing a smug grin. "Then by all means, proceed."

I bit down hard in the inside of my cheek to keep from crying out as the blade pierced my skin. A trickle of blood trailed down my neck, and my heart pounded. *One. Two. Three. Four. Five.* No one moved. Heaven against hell. Evil verses eviler. And me, stuck in the middle of it all. God, if there was one, sure had a fucked up sense of humor.

Falel acted first. He propelled himself forward, crashing into the group of demons like a bowling ball headed for the perfect strike. They scattered and the room erupted in battle. Mishca screamed, a string of syllables I didn't understand. She jerked me backward and launched herself into the fray to join her partner.

As the two groups clashed, I inched to the left, trying to find a clear path to the stairs. But every time I made a move, the battle would overflow, sealing me in. Bodies flew, so did curses, and the entire house seemed to shake. It was impossible to cut a path through the swath of destruction they carved.

Considering it was five against two, Mishca and Falel held their own. Falel took down two demons, his blade dripping with blood and gore. He stopped for a moment to take a triumphant breath, then rushed to help Mishca, but he was too focused on her. He was taken down by a blade through the back of his head, dealt by the tallest demon. His body fell to the ground, eyes frozen in surprise, the sound of it lost to the chaos.

Upon seeing her comrade fall, Mishca let out an otherworldly howl. She'd taken out one of the demons on her own, but was now caught, restrained by one at each arm.

"You should have retreated when we offered you the chance, angel." The tall demon gave a dark laugh. It placed a hand on either side of her head and pushed her to her knees.

They were going to kill her, but there was nothing I could do. Not that she would have deserved my help anyway, after everything she did to me. With the battle all but over, and the remaining demons focused on Mishca, I eased out of my safe corner and inched toward the staircase. I didn't even make it three steps.

"Where do you think you're going?" The tall one growled. He towered over me, lips pulled back to reveal a toothy grin. "We're here to rescue you."

"Really," I said, chancing a sideways glance at Mishca and the other demon. She was still on her knees, with the demon's hand around her neck. I took a step away. "And who's going to save me from you?"

His hand shot out and closed around my upper arm, clamping down with brutal force. I bit back a gasp. "Lord Azirak sent us."

Great. The demonic cavalry. Except I was pretty sure they were anything but. If they were, in fact, Azirak's demons, then they were acting on their own. That, or…

Acid bubbled up in my stomach and I swallowed back a rush of bile. What if Azirak *had* sent them? Did that mean Jax found Malphi? That she'd gotten to him?

"My name is Karak." The demon gave a slight bow and winked. His grip around my arm tightened as he dragged me toward the stairs. "Come. Your presence is needed elsewhere."

As we reached the middle of the stairs, there was a brutal whooshing sound. Mishca's blade, brandished by the last remaining demon, sliced through the air. A sick sound, muffled and wet, followed by a thud. The angel's head hit the concrete, eyes open and mouth frozen in a silent scream.

As Karak finished dragging me up the steps, I choked back a mouthful of vomit, knowing that moment would stay with me for the rest of my life.

However long that might be.

Chapter Twenty-Seven

JAX

An hour. Sixty fucking minutes. That's how long we'd sat there, just staring at each other. "My patience is officially gone," I growled, finally standing. "If there's something you need me to do, get on with it then take me to Malphi."

Ranook opened its mouth, then closed it. A disturbing grin followed. It cocked its head, seemingly listening to something. I focused and heard it too. A car door in the driveway.

"The wait is over," the demon said, standing. Four strides and it was at the door. A second later, the entryway burst open.

There was a commotion followed by a small form stumbling over the threshold. Sam. Two other demons followed, forcing her inside and to the floor at my feet. The sight of her, helpless on the floor and in such a submissive position caused my demon to bristle with excitement. I felt it, an exhilarating awareness of the power just within its grasp. While it turned my stomach, I had no choice other than to go with it. "Kneel in our lord's presence!"

The scent of blood filled the air. Hers. Nothing fatal. The wounds were superficial. But someone had hurt her. Caused her pain. A part of me knew I should be enraged. That I should be swinging blindly at anything that moved in an attempt to make them all pay. But I wasn't. I didn't. The rage was there, bubbling and potent and barely contained, but my breathing was even. My pulse in check.

"Samantha Merrick," I said, dropping down so that we were eye to eye. Moving felt strange. It was me, yet it wasn't. I was in control, and yet I was helpless. Both the marionette and the puppeteer at the same time.

To prove to myself that I would be able to do what needed to be done, I stood. Making a fist, I punched outward, clocking the nearest demon—a tall, blond fucker with beady eyes and a crooked nose. He went down hard, surprised, as I rounded on the second. A single blow to the center of his neck sent him sprawling back, choking for air.

That's how it all went in my mind. In reality, I hadn't touched a soul. I was still kneeling in front of Sam, watching her with concern and unparalleled hunger.

"They have done you harm." My voice was cold. Clinical. My arms reached for her. Even though it wasn't me—she had to know that—when she cringed away, it stung. Azi was unaffected, though. It pushed forward, slipping my arms beneath her legs and behind her head, lifting her from the floor. "Do not worry. We will make them pay," it said, laying her on the couch.

Tense, Sam looked around the room, her gaze landing on each demon in turn. The two that brought her in, then Ranook, finally settling on me. "Jax," she said. There was a spark of fear in her eyes. It killed me to see, but at the same time, sent a ripple of excitement surging through my system. With a deep breath, I tasted it. Sweet. Seductive. A spike of gray wafted from her shoulders, lingering in the air for a moment before dissipating. "I want to talk to Jax."

I wanted to tell her that she *was* talking to me, to give her a sign that this was all an act, part of my master plan. But I wasn't sure I believed it. Control kept oscillating. One second it was me, the next it was the demon, the change so eerily seamless that I could no longer tell who was in control at any given moment.

"What's the hold up?" the smaller of the two demons that had come in with Sam snarled. "Claim the bitch and let's get this moving." It flexed the fingers on its right hand and flashed a predatory grin. "I want to stretch my legs."

My body was across the room in a flash. I had the offender against the wall, suspended in midair by my fists, all in a single beat of the human heart. "You will contain yourself or I will break you in half."

The other demon's fear flooded the room, and the sensation it brought—the sickest, most electric feeling—obscured everything. It was the best high coupled with the most sensual encounter of my life. I was instantly hard. Excited. Charged and ready to take on anything from heaven to hell. I didn't care what Azi did with my body. It didn't matter who it hurt or what the demon destroyed. As long as this feeling never faded.

Slowly, I set the offending demon down. "Leave us."

"Lord Azirak." Ranook started forward. "Considering the history between the two humans—"

"LEAVE US," I roared. The sound shook the walls and rattled the glass.

The three demons cringed and inched toward the door. "As you wish, my lord. But know that I will have your guard stationed at all exits." They scurried out of sight.

I settled into the chair across from Sam and sighed, struck by the strangeness of the sound. Me, yet not. Still heady from the fear though, I didn't care. There was nothing wrong with this. Things were as they were meant to be. Azirak and I shared this body. We shared a common goal.

"We have a problem," I said.

"Please," Sam begged. She leaned forward. "Let me talk to Jax. Get me the hell out of here. The cuff—" With a sharp inhalation, she doubled over, arms wrapped tight around herself.

"You're in pain."

She nodded without looking up.

"The cuff's power has almost come to fruition."

She lifted her head, gaze locking on mine. It stirred something deep in my gut. A spark of…of what? Something about this wasn't right. We should leave. I knew there was a reason, but as hard as I chased the thought, it stayed just out of reach. Uncatchable.

"It's going to kill me. If we don't find Malphi and get Chase to remove it, I'm going to *die*."

A wave of sadness came on strong, but dissipated. "I can make it stop. I can remove the cuff."

Her skin paled. "You—" She jumped from the couch.

"I am Jax, Sammy. I'm also Azirak. Trust us."

"No!" She tossed her head and let out an anguished cry. A moment later she launched herself off the couch at me. "You're not the same. Give him back to me! You promised."

"It's time you stopped viewing us as separate entities." I stepped to the side, grabbing her around the waist as she flew past. It was strange to see the contrast, pale skin against my darker complexion. Delicate and breakable. So breakable… "If you allow me to claim you, I will have the power to remove the cuff. The pain will end."

I let her go and she stumbled away. "Go to hell."

"You have no choice. Allow me to claim you. I swear on my royal blood that no harm will ever befall you."

She stumbled away, shaking her head. "Royal blood? You don't have royal blood." Legs spread, like she was preparing for a fight, she said, "Get over this, Jax. You're in there. I know it. You would never let them take me."

"This is a complicated situation. I understand your confusion, and I sympathize. You must know that is unprecedented. My kind, we care not for the fates of humans. But you... My concern for you..."

"If you care about me, then get me the hell out of here."

"What you ask is impossible. Even if I conspired to remove you from this place, the others would never allow it. Your fragile body would be mortally damaged in our attempt."

"Bullshit," she spat.

"Please. You have little time left. I do not wish to see you expire. I—" My body stiffened. A new presence—not here, but close—set my insides on fire. "Malphi is near."

"Good," Sam cried, throwing herself forward again. She grasped my hands and squeezed tight. "I know you're in there, Jax. Kill Malphi and let's get the hell out of here!"

There was a spike of rage. I pushed her. She flew back, landing on the couch with jarring force. The spark grew bigger, and some of the haze lifted. Sam. Sam shouldn't be here. Not like this...

My shoulders rolled and a deep breath filled my lungs. No. She belonged here, exactly like this. With me. "Do not speak like that again. Malphi is *mine*. As you are. No harm will come to her. Or to you."

"So you're saying you love us both?" The venom in her voice needled something deep in me. It chased the spark of consciousness and battled the haze, but wasn't strong enough. "Because, I don't know about your demon-bitch, but I don't like sharing."

"Love." The word felt strange as it slipped across my lips. Wrong in so many ways, but right in one. My head moved up and down, slowly. "Yes. I *love* you both."

"I call bullshit again," Sam growled, then cringed. She gasped, twisting the edge of the couch cushion in her palm. "I—oh God."

"Time slips away. I can offer relief and safety. Zenak will never again darken your world."

Her eyes squeezed closed. A thin layer of sweat had broken out on her skin, glistening as a single drop trailed down the side of her face. The exertion was too much for a mortal. It wouldn't be long now.

"You want my power to kill Chase. You know what will happen if you're all freed," she rasped. "Everything—Earth, humans, all life in general—will be destroyed."

"I am...undecided about Zenak's fate. I wish to restore the clan, but I can foresee complications. However, the power you contain must not be claimed by our enemies. To ensure that, I must obtain it."

She laughed, disbelieving and desperate, then she gritted her teeth as a whimper followed. It disturbed me to see her in such pain, and I moved to comfort her, but something stopped me. A familiar presence, dark and sensual—one my body desired and my essence remembered in excruciating detail.

The door behind us creaked open. The scent of her filled the air and, like a physical blow, nearly brought me to my knees. I turned and she was there, with her long legs and wild, raven-colored hair, filling up every inch of the doorway.

"My love," a familiar voice said. She winked. The hum of power filled the room. With each step, the memory of our previous times together grew sharper. I recalled the first time I saw her—both in hell, and here, on Earth. The cuts and bruises from a few days ago had faded from her face, and the limp was gone.

The haze keeping me trapped shifted, and a moment of clarity slammed through me. It brought with it conflicting emotions, most of which I didn't understand. But there was one that rang fierce, stood out strong and blazing. *Rage.* For an instant I was able to push Azirak aside. I lunged for her, pushing her hard against the wall and pinning her there, hands tight around her neck. Betrayal burned, a single ember fanning into an inferno, and all I wanted was to feel her blood on my hands. "Malphi…"

Chapter Twenty-Eight

I'd heard him wrong. That was the only logical explanation. This woman wasn't Malphi. She couldn't be.

In the doorway stood a familiar, black-haired witch. A boyfriend coveting, manipulating woman who'd forced Jax's hand and tied them together, inserting herself into his life in hopes that she would get what she wanted. Power? Him?

But if she was a demon—Azirak's demonic booty call— wouldn't *Jax* have known? Wouldn't he have taken Sadie Gray out right when this all started? He certainly would have never linked them.

Jax flew at her, fingers hooked and ready, but he didn't follow through. He had her against the wall by the neck, had *Malphi* pinned, but hadn't moved to finish the job yet.

She chuckled and gently eased him away. With a wink at me, she slung her arm around his shoulder and licked the side of his face slowly, starting at the tip of his chin then running her tongue up his cheek and down again, finishing by biting at his top lip.

Jax simply stood there. Staring at her like she wasn't real. I didn't know if it was because Azi was happy to see her, or if Jax was in as much shock as I was, but it scared me. The almost vacant, desperate look in his eyes. They weren't solid black like they had been a few minutes ago, but they weren't thinly rimmed with a gray center, either. I had no idea which one of them was in control.

"I bet you have a ton of questions," she said, turning back to me.

I gritted my teeth and held my breath. With each inhalation, the pain thrived. The cuff was like liquid fire against my skin now.

"How is this possible?" Jax asked. His voice was slightly off key. Deeper than normal and laced with a chill. "I linked to this human body. I did not feel you."

Sadie—*Malphi*—gave a throaty chuckle. "I was fortunate enough to be born into the body of a witch this go-around. Her bloodline is very powerful." She sighed. "But, as you know, part of our banishment was the removal of all power. I was born into the body of a witch, yet had no access to the goods, if you know what I'm saying."

"But you do have magic," I insisted.

She laughed again and shrugged. With a quick move of her hand, she reached beneath her shirt and pulled out a long chain. On the end dangled a bright red stone. The one Chase wanted! "This is a powerful stone, created in the fires of our home. You don't recall, but the Brim Stone was smuggled here eons ago, by your hand, my lord. I was able to use it to tap in to the bloodline's power. I cloaked myself, and those loyal to me, so you wouldn't see me coming." She began to pace. "Of course, I was a bit pissed when you didn't recognize me after linking us. It made me testy."

Azi, now in control, lifted Jax's hand to her face, a tender gesture that incited a raging spark of jealousy in me. It wasn't Jax really, but seeing his hands on another woman stole the air from my lungs. "But why?" he asked. "Why hide from me? Why not reveal yourself?"

Her expression darkened. She flicked a finger in my direction. "Because of that *thing*. Your human half is so enamored with it. It clouds your judgment and snares you with humanity. It keeps you tethered. I knew you would never take Zenak's life. If I revealed myself to you, I would have been in danger, not only from our enemies, but from your human."

"It is true that I struggled with my task. But the reasons are not as simple as you state."

"Yes," she purred, running her hand across his cheek and down to his shoulder. Skimming her nails across his arm, she said, "They are. Mate with me. Consummate our union and I will do the task for you. Once I am of royal blood, the weight will not fall on your shoulders alone. It will be my…gift to you."

Her hands dropped to the button of Jax's jeans, deftly slipping it through the hole. When there was no protest, she raked her fingers up his chest, across the thin material of his T-shirt. Gripping it at the neck, she ripped it like tissue paper, the remnants slipping from his shoulders and falling to the floor at their feet.

"Jax," I cried. I wasn't sure what scared me more. Having to watch the only man I'd ever loved have sex with another woman right in front of me, or the world-shattering chaos that would come as a result of it. "Don't let them do this. It's your body! Take control of it."

Sadie howled—a vicious, angry sound—as she launched herself at me. She grabbed my wrist, squeezing so hard that I was positive my hand would pop off. "That fool Zenak gambled on the human's love for you. But he should have known better. My lord would have never allowed harm to come to me!"

"Jax, do—"

She grabbed my chin with her free hand and squeezed, nails digging in and breaking the skin. "I'll enjoy watching you squirm as he takes me." She leaned closer. All I could see was the dark onyx of her irises. "And then take pleasure in the pain you feel as you die."

Malphi jerked me across the floor and forced me down at Jax's feet. She grabbed a handful of my hair and gave a vicious twist. "Feed, my lord. Take in her anguish and pain. Then take me and we will claim her together. The power will enable us to destroy our enemies and take our rightful place in this world and the next."

It was Jax's face that looked down at me, but his eyes were like Sadie's. Solid and soulless. "Allow me to claim you. I will remain true to my word. No harm will ever come to you." Azi lifted me off the ground. "I will make it painless." Ebony eyes skimmed the length of my body, catching on my chest for a moment before settling on my lips. "Pleasurable, even."

The demon leaned in and brushed the softest of kisses across my forehead. I froze, too terrified to even breathe.

"What are you doing?" Malphi bellowed. It wrenched me backward and I stumbled, falling onto the coffee table. It cracked in half. Splinters and pieces of wood littered the floor. "You owe her no mercy. Claim her by force."

"I am fond of the human and will cause her no unnecessary pain."

"Fond?" Malphi screamed. "You're *fond* of it?"

That answered that. Apparently the demoness wasn't the sharing type.

"I demand that you claim it. Claim it and kill it. We have no use for it."

With each moment, she grew angrier and angrier. Her

fury was terrifying, but I also saw it as a possible opportunity. Struggling to my feet, trying to push away the crushing pain from the cuff, I said, "I'll consider it, but I have a condition."

Azi's eyes met mine and I suppressed a shiver. "What do you wish, Samantha Merrick?" It sighed. "Sammy…"

This was a dangerous plan, considering how Malphi reacted to even the lightest show of kindness by Azirak, but I was out of options. The cuff was close to killing me. I had moments left. I still wasn't convinced, even if this worked, that it would save my life. Even if we managed to take Malphi down, how could I get to Chase in time?

"You won't let me speak to Jax." I took a step forward. "I know that. But physically, you're him."

"More than that," the demon said. It followed my every move, gaze all but devouring me. "We are the same. I feel his desire as he feels mine."

I fought a shiver and snuck a peek at Sadie… Malphi. Her lips were mashed in a thin line, and judging by her body language, there was very little keeping her from ripping out my throat. Good. "Then kiss me. You can take away the pain, make this pleasurable? Prove it. Show me."

Fire sparked in those inky black eyes and the demon wasted no time. It crossed to me in two long strides, gathering me into Jax's arms. The kiss was like an internal meltdown. Basic and primal. Vehement and possessive. Azirak wound Jax's hands through my hair, fingers tangling around large sections and tugging forcefully. It murmured something inaudible, dropping Jax's hands down to my waist for a moment before slipping them to cup my backside. A second later my legs were around his waist.

An unearthly roar shattered the room. My head snapped back, and the warmth from Jax's body disappeared, replaced by sharp pain as Malphi dragged me backward. "You dare to take this wretched creature in front of me? Before consummating *our* union?"

"You will release Samantha Merrick," Jax said, voice like ice.

Malphi laughed, the sound like scraping rusted metal. Harsh. Angry. Unforgiving. "Do you favor this insect over me, my lord?"

"I favor her." It was very matter of fact. "Not above you. I believe—I believe I favor her the same as you. She is *mine*."

Malphi's face twisted into a mask of rage. Her fingers closed around my neck, and the pressure increased. "That is the human stain speaking!"

I gasped. The pain from the cuff was nearly blinding now, a red hot poker jabbing at me from the inside. My legs were numb. Even if the demoness were to let go, I wasn't confident that I could run away.

Her hand tightened. "You must choose—this abomination or me!"

"You are rash," Azi said, still eerily calm. It came a step closer. "As you have always been. But this will not aid our cause."

"Our cause?" She shook me. "This is not about our cause. You have no intention of destroying Zenak." Her grip loosened and her voice became somewhat softer. She sighed, looking and sounding more like the simply annoying witch I knew and hated. "I have seen it grow worse in you over the centuries, Azirak. It's a disease. One I will free you from. We will claim the Pure and kill it. Then we will mate and I will kill Zenak."

My breathing grew labored. The rasping as my lungs fought to fill with air echoed in my ears.

"I will not say this again, Malphi. Release her unharmed." I could see it in his eyes. Jax was in there. He was fighting. Unfortunately it seemed as though it would be a losing battle.

"Who do you prefer?" Malphi demanded. She gave me

another furious jostle.

"I desire you both." Azi's confusion grew. "Is this a problem? Did we not have multiple consorts in hell?"

"This thing is more than a consort to you," she growled. "It is more than a source of power. You—" She choked on the rest of the sentence before trying again. "You *love* it."

The demon came several steps closer to where we stood. "By human definition, I love you as well."

Malphi's face contorted. "By *human definition*?" She shook me again. "You are a royal. A god among our kind. Finish this and take your rightful place!"

The expression on Jax's expression was thoughtful. Azi remained where it was, gaze alternating between Malphi and me. She took it as a green light. Turning me to face her, eyes raging with madness, she said, "The cuff is about to kill you. This is your last chance. Agree to be claimed or die."

My body was mostly numb now, the strange, intense pain radiating from inside me the only thing left. I didn't feel Malphi's hand around my neck, and the only indication that she was squeezing off my air was the difficulty I had filling my lungs.

But for some reason, I was unafraid.

A thought sparked, deep in the back of my mind. An ember that bloomed into a raging inferno. In an instant my outlook changed. The mere possibility of hope kept me balanced on the edge, not alive, but not yet dead. It was that moment that brought clarity. The answer to my current predicament was suddenly so incredibly clear.

I turned my head so that Malphi and I were face to face. "Fine," I said, my voice eerily calm. Somehow I knew, deep down, that it was too late to save my life, but I could still stop them from making my last moments torture. I could have the last word. "I agree to be claimed—by myself."

Chapter Twenty-Nine

AZIRAK/JAX

Everything went silent. There was a static in the air, coupled with the fury radiating from Malphi. The muddled colors that surrounded Sam dispersed, leaving an emptiness that needled the deepest parts of me. Of all of me.

A scream filled the room. The human girl, Samantha Merrick's—Sammy's—eyes rolled back, then closed. The sound of her breathing ceased.

Malphi let the body fall to the floor and stepped away. "You have damned us," she spat, turning on me. "Your diseased human half has betrayed us."

Something built inside me. I ignored my mate and focused again on the girl, so small and still, lying at my feet. Her lack of movement, of vitality, only added to the turbulent force stirring.

"Have you nothing to say?" Malphi shouted. "No words to defend yourself?"

There were words. Things I wanted to say. Feelings I

needed to somehow express. *Human emotions.* But they were buried. Bogged down by the weight of the massive force building inside me. My human, Jax, was silent as well. I felt his sorrow, a nearly overpowering boulder that threatened to crush all that I was. I shared his pain and found myself surprised that it was not only for the loss of power, but for the girl. A human woman.

Sammy...

Hands gripped my shoulders and spun my body around. Malphi and I were face to face. "This is salvageable," she growled and began to unbutton my pants. "We will consummate and I will destroy Zenak."

She slid her hands up my chest, then threaded them through my hair. Warm lips caressed a trail up my neck. The sensation was anything but pleasurable. The stink of lust turned my gut. I shifted my head, gaze finding the girl again. As Malphi did her best to further her cause, my attention would not be torn from the woman on the floor.

It wasn't long before Malphi noticed.

"That bitch is dead at our feet and you're still infested with affection for it?"

Again, I wanted to respond. Again, sound failed me.

This enraged my mate. She pushed me away, the fire behind her eyes turning from passion to fury. "Have you forgotten?" She took a menacing step forward. "All that I've done for you? The things I've endured over the course of a millennium?"

Still, I had nothing to say. The woman still filled my view. The feeling in my gut grew stronger.

"I suffered for you. Endured years of torment by Zenak's own hand. I watched you cavort with humans lifetime after lifetime in an attempt to make me pay for my disobedience by taking retribution on our enemy. Now we find ourselves on the verge of victory, you focus not on me, but a dead human?

Explain yourself!"

"You are mine," I said, eyes still on the girl. "As she was his."

"That's your answer?" Malphi raged. "That is supposed to justify your lack of action?"

"It is meant to justify nothing. My words are merely an explanation." I lifted my head to study her. "I began a war for you, my love. The result of that action found us removed from our home. Ejected and sentenced to mediocrity for all eternity. How is it that you find yourself able to question my affections?"

Some of her rage subsided. "Your infatuation with that bitch sours me."

"It is not infatuation. It is as unbreakable a bond as you and I share. It—" Movement on the floor captured my attention once again.

The softest sound filled the room—a single breath pulled between soft lips, followed by a faint metallic clink. The demon cuff fell to the ground. Malphi noticed at the same time I did. "No!" she screamed, and dove for Sam.

The murderous intent in her eyes freed the building force inside me. Watching Malphi drag Sam off the ground and throw her around like a ragdoll was the final push I needed.

I burst through the invisible bonds keeping me trapped and regained control over my body. I moved knowing that there was only one goal, one endgame.

Sam.

Winding my hands around a hank of the demoness's hair, I hauled it backward. She wailed in pain, then lashed out, raking its nails across my cheek. "Bastard!"

"Let it go," I snapped. Sam stirred, but hadn't opened her

eyes yet. The fact I could hear her breathing, though, steady and strong, was all I needed. Leaving the demoness alive was stupid. A fucking disaster in the making. But I couldn't kill it in cold blood. I'd lost Sam twice now. As much as I hated Azirak, it *was* a part of me. It always would be. Its anger was my anger, its struggles mine. A part of me feared what Malphi's death would do to me.

"I won't hurt you," I told the demoness. "Just leave us alone. There will be other lives. Other chances. Wait it out and try again."

Malphi stared at me, expression unreadable, its human eyes—Sadie's eyes—sparking with something I didn't quite understand. It—she—I was so fucking confused—shifted from foot to foot, alternating between me and Sam. I thought it was over. That Malphi would turn and walk the other way.

I was wrong.

The female demon let out a horrible scream and lunged for Sam. Closer by a couple of feet, it reached her first. There was no plan behind my actions. No thought other than the threat posed to the woman I loved. My hand grasped the end table, fingers closing around the first thing they connected with. A ballpoint pen. Without hesitation, I charged Malphi, wrapping one arm around the front of its neck, then plunging the tip of the pen in with the other.

Malphi stumbled back, crashing into me. I caught the demoness before it hit the ground, cradling its head as it fell. A series of coughs followed, and the demoness tried to speak, but only blood came out. I felt the instant Sadie's human heart stopped. Malphi's essence exploded from the body, hovering for a moment above our heads before shooting away. Off to be reborn? Who the fuck knew. All that mattered was that for this lifetime, Sam would be safe.

Sam stirred again, and all I wanted was to go to her. To wrap her in my arms and inhale her sweet, familiar scent.

But I couldn't move. I couldn't even breathe. A heaviness had settled in my limbs and all feeling drained away. I knew what was coming, and I had no regrets. I would have gladly sacrificed myself, everything that I was or would ever be, for Samantha Merrick.

"Sammy, I love —"

Chapter Thirty

My eyelids were leaden, and despite the pressure at my throat and weightless feeling beneath my feet, I couldn't force them open. There was a change in the room. I felt something shift, and it was that transition that enabled me to finally open my eyes.

I was alive. The demon cuff lay in two pieces on the floor to my right. The only reminder was what resembled a burn scar where it had rested against my skin.

I'd been claimed. Not by heaven or hell, but by earth. By myself. I hadn't known what to expect, or if it would even work, but it surprised me that I didn't feel any different. There was no power surging through my body. No otherworldly thoughts in my head. I was simply me. Sam Merrick. The same girl who always forgot to turn off the lights and never filled the gas tank until the car was on fumes. A visionless slacker with no career goals and no cash.

But I was alive. And so was Jax.

Jax.

I turned to see him sitting a few feet away, Sadie Gray's body cradled in his lap. He watched her for a moment, his expression sad, then lifted his gaze to meet mine. I could no longer feel him. The link, however I'd created it in the first place, was gone.

"Malphi is dead," he announced. His voice was strange. Deeper and just a little bit broken, which made no sense.

Why would he care if she was dead? Upon closer inspection, I noticed his eyes kept flickering. Gray. Black. Gray. Black. I counted five switches before it stopped, irises settling on the color of midnight.

"It is only fair that he goes with her."

A wave of icy fear rolled over me. "He?"

"Your human ended this life for her. I may not have the ability to end his without bringing about my own demise, but I can lock his essence away."

"You—"

Azirak moved Sadie's body aside, gently setting it on the carpet before standing. "Retribution. Payment. A life for a life."

"No," I cried, and scrambled upright. Tears burned my eyes. "If you can't take his life, then take mine. Let him go."

It was Jax's face looking down on me, but the expression of pity was foreign. "His affection makes it impossible for me to act against you—and I have no desire to see you physically harmed. Your power has been claimed, but you can still be an asset."

The words sent an entirely new kind of chill dancing along my spine. "Only the person who claimed my power can use it. Since that's me, I'm betting you're shit out of luck," I snapped. Anger burned hot. "What's to stop me from making you give him back?" I advanced several steps. "If my power is the most sought after thing in heaven and hell, then I'll just *make* you return him to me."

Azirak laughed. "Any harm done to me will be done to him. Attempt to make me relinquish control and you will destroy this body, and the human along with me. Choose your actions with care."

"He speaks the truth," a new voice said. I whirled to the doorway where Heckle stood watching us. "Jax is gone."

"*You!*" I roared. "You lied to us. Tricked us." The sound of his voice, the look on his face—everything about Heckle incited my fury. I started for him, eager to test that destruction theory, but froze halfway across the room.

"Careful, Sam," he said. "While you now have an unprecedented edge, there are still some things that remain untouchable."

I took a deep breath. Azirak bowed once to me, then turned and bowed to Heckle. Without a word, it slipped through the door, leaving us alone.

"Fix this," I spat. "Do something to help Jax."

"There is nothing I can do. His punishment brings balance for your life."

My legs grew rubbery, and with a sob, I collapsed to the floor. This wasn't happening. He couldn't be gone.

"I warned you that the bond would end in tragedy. Because of his tie to you, he was able to overcome Azirak's hold long enough to kill Malphi."

"The alternative was for me to die," I bit back. "How the fuck is that any better?"

"Did you ever stop to think that maybe one of you was fated to die?"

"But no one died," I said. Jax was my past. He was my present, and goddammit, he was my future. I had no intention of giving up on him. My previous experience proved that even death wasn't final…and Jax wasn't dead. He was still in there, with Azirak. "Jax is technically still alive."

Heckle cocked a brow, but didn't answer.

No. "There's a way to fix this. An alternate path to take."

More silence.

Heckle frowned. His expression was a mix of certainty and bleak resignation. "There's always an alternate path to take, Sam. But as I've said before, some road blocks require a sacrifice to remove."

Sacrifice? I'd already lost everything. What the hell else was there? "Tell me," I said, climbing to my feet again. "Tell me how to get him back."

He didn't look like he wanted to tell me, but he had to know I'd never let it go. Not when Jax was at stake. After a long moment—one of the longest of my life—Heckle sighed. "The only way for him to come back now is for Azirak to allow it. The demon must leave him willingly."

"Leave him?" I swallowed my surprise. "As in, there's a way to separate them?"

Heckle smiled. Then he turned on his heel and, without a word, walked out the door.

Keep reading for a preview of *Released*, book 3 in the Eternal Balance series

Chapter One

S he hadn't left my side in days. Sam Merrick, the girl with fury in her eyes and unrelenting determination in her soul.

I could hear her heartbeat from across the room. As she approached, a noxious scent filled the air, followed by a plate thrust into my face. "Eat it," she demanded.

Azirak took it from her and placed it on the bar in front of me. Human food was offensive to the demon living inside me. The one currently in control of my body. It survived on the darker side of human emotion—not cheeseburgers. "No. It has an unpleasant odor."

I couldn't really argue. Food at the Viking wasn't fit for human—or demon—consumption.

Sam made a sound like a growl and kicked the edge of my chair. I felt the vibration, but it was faraway and detached. "Does it look like I care?" she said. "Hold his damn nose and stuff it down his throat." The girl on the other side of the bar, a dark skinned woman with multiple colors in her hair, watched us with a strange expression.

Azi studied the burger. Under his command, my finger poked at the meat, and I felt a ripple of disgust go through me. "Why?"

Sam's skin took on a reddish hue and the muscles in her neck tightened. Sweet-tasting anger, a red haze that rolled off her in waves, made my mouth water. "Because he needs to eat!"

Just eat the fucking thing, I said. I was locked inside my own body, punishment for killing Malphi, Azi's mate. I couldn't communicate with Sam, but I could still annoy the shit out of the demon. *She won't give up until you do.*

It pushed me back and lifted my head to meet her gaze. The fury there was enough to rival any demon tenfold. A swell of admiration washed over me. Azi often wondered what kind of a demon Sam would have made. "So long as I continue to feed he will be nourished."

She stood her ground, glaring like she wanted to rip me apart. I knew the contempt wasn't for me, but I still hated seeing it. Hated what this all was doing to her. "His body needs actual *food*." Leaning in close, she added, "Not other people's bad vibes."

We've been over this. Unless you want us to shrivel up, my body needs food.

Azi growled and snatched the burger from the plate. Weakness, considering recent events, could get us killed. It could get Sam killed, and strangely, the demon didn't want that.

It stuffed the overcooked animal into my mouth, eating it in three bites. It was dry, and the texture was unpleasant. "Thank you," she ground out, as though the words caused her physical pain. She reached around the bar to grab her coat. "Now, are you ready to go?"

I stood and, giving the plate one last glare, said, "I am."

She led the way, weaving through the diminishing crowd of Viking employees. It was four a.m. and the club was closing. Since the demon had totaled our only ride a week ago, we had a long walk ahead of us.

Heading out the back door and into the alley next to the club, Sam pulled her coat tighter. She looked one way, and then the other. Satisfied that we were alone, she started forward. I followed, thankful that Azi remained silent.

She didn't care for it when the demon spoke to her. She hadn't said it, but it was obvious by the pain in her eyes every time it opened my mouth. It was my voice, the sound eerily familiar, and yet different. Azi had no desire to cause her more suffering than it already had, so the demon kept to itself unless addressed directly.

There was a chill in the air, and several blocks from the club, it began to rain, which was unfortunate. For the last block or so, something had been following us. The storm would make it harder to track the scent.

As we passed a row of shops, I picked up the scent again. This time it was closer—and definitely not human. My fingers closed around Sam's wrist, and, without explanation, Azi dragged her into the small space between two of the buildings.

"What the hell are you—"

It covered her mouth and leaned close. For a moment, the smell of her overrode my senses and sent a powerful spark of desire to my core. One of the drawbacks to being locked in here was that with the demon in the driver's seat, each sensation was magnified. It inhaled, savoring the sudden spike of anger, and grinned when the smallest tuft of lust seeped through.

"Be still and stay silent," it whispered against her ear. My lips brushed the edge and a wave of longing rolled over me. I wanted to tell Sam I missed her, to let her know that I would find a way out of this. But no matter how loud I roared, she wouldn't hear me. It was the demon's words that came from my lips. "We are being followed."

The alley was devoid of light, but my senses were inhuman. I saw every detail of her face, from the worried gleam in her eyes to the sudden tension in her body. She gave a slight nod and Azi removed my hand from her mouth.

Get Sammy out of there, I growled. I fought for dominance, failed, then let out an enraged yell. *If anything happens to her…*

"We will be fine." The demon's assurance was for both of us.

Movement on the street distracted it momentarily, and a large black blur flew at us from the far end of the alley. Azi pushed Sam to the ground as the hulking mass crashed into me.

Growling filled the air. The creature perched on my chest snarled, viscous black fluid oozing from between rows of jagged red teeth. I knew what it was because Azi did—a carnivus, a vicious dog-like thing from the depths of hell, used as frontline soldiers in war.

"Impossible," Azi said, greeting the beast with a snarl of its own. It gripped the thing's head on both sides and hefted away with as much force as my body could muster. I was far stronger than other humans, but still had limitations. Matching the strength of a full-grown carnivus was definitely one of them.

"Hey," Sam called. The sound was followed almost immediately by a large object hurdling my way. It connected with the beast's head, eliciting a savage howl. The pressure against Azi's grip vanished and the carnivus whirled and charged. "Shit!" she mumbled before scattering in the opposite direction.

Get up, I snapped. *That thing is going to rip her to fucking shreds!*

Azi leaped to my feet and sprang into action. A rush of fury poured from the demon and my body soared over the charging beast and landed in a graceful crouch a few feet in front of Sam. Whirling, it faced the charging bastard just as the thing pounced.

Crashing together in midair, the demon twisted with a violent jerk and redirected the carnivus sideways, toward the wall. The thing collided with the brick, a thundering crash echoing through the small space.

The carnivus climbed to its feet, scaly hackles rising. Azi positioned us protectively in front of Sam, bracing my body for another round. But the carnivus didn't attack. It matched our steps—us back, it forward—but made no move to instigate more violence.

"Get rid of it," Azi snarled at Sam.

She made a choking sound. "Get rid— How? Am I supposed to offer it a cookie or something? Give it a damn belly rub? You get rid of it. *You're* the demon badass."

"You're a Pure," Azi fired back, my voice laced with venom. The demon's patience was waning, but underneath that, I felt concern. The carnivus was, unlike other things, a very real threat—one that shouldn't exist outside hell. "You are unbound. Use your energy."

The canine-like creature snarled and snapped its massive jaw, but still made no advance. "What's it waiting for?" Sam gripped the back of my shirt. I felt her fingers skim my skin as they wrapped themselves around the thin fabric.

"These are not creatures known for their intelligence. They are soldiers, bound by the commands of their masters." However this thing came to be here, it couldn't have been acting on its own. Azi was very familiar with them, having used the monsters in its own army. That made me an expert as well. These things had brains the size of horses.

"It isn't acting of its own free will," a man said from

behind the beast. He emerged from the shadows, approaching as though he didn't have a care in the world.

The carnivus froze, its low-throated rumble silenced.

"Abel." Azi pushed the word past my lips as if it left a bad taste in my mouth. "Your timing is impeccable."

The man gave a small bow. "Azirak. Please, call me Heckle." He nodded to Sam as well.

She sprang from behind me and eyed the carnivus with caution. "Where the hell have you been? I've been trying to find you for over a week now."

Heckle's eyebrows lifted. He looked down at the carnivus, then back to her. "For?"

Anger seeped into the air. Waves of red smoke that sent shivers of excitement through my body. "The last thing you said to me was that there was a way to separate Jax and Azi. Then *poof.* You dropped off the face of the planet."

"As I recall, it was you who said that. I never confirmed it."

The red smoke thickened and Sam clenched her fists tight. The demon was amused. It wanted to see what would happen if she struck Heckle. "You implied it," she said. Her voice was deadly, and the sound of it stirred something primal in Azi. The demon took a step forward, moving closer to her.

Heckle sighed. "As I said, Azirak would have to leave of its own accord." He glanced toward me. "Is that a possibility?"

A rush of images flashed before me, a swarm of pictures involving the witch, Sadie Gray—also known as Malphi, Azi's mate. They ended with one of me, wide eyed and furious, standing over her corpse. "No," the demon said. The tone left no room for argument. No room for forgiveness.

"Then this conversation is moot." Heckle folded his arms. "I have a task for you. Something suited for your particular talents."

"A task?" Sam balked. "Are you high? It's your fault I

have a permanent supernatural target pinned to my back. Because of you, I have to sleep with one eye open, and Jax—"

"Enough," Heckle said. He appeared calm, but Azi sensed an underlying storm. "You belong to me. Both of you. You each made a bargain and you will fill your end of it."

"I made no bargain with you," Azi said calmly.

"But the body you're currently residing in did. Therefore, you are bound by Jax's word."

I took satisfaction from the demon's ire. Keep me locked away in my own body? Well, fuck you.

Suck it up. I gave him my word. His help in exchange for service. Nothing you can do about it.

But the demon didn't see it that way. Fury filled me, simmering rage barely contained. My hand came up, wrapping tightly around Heckle's neck. "You dare conspire to enslave a royal of hell?"

Heckle was silent for a minute. He blinked once. Twice. Then with a sigh, he pried my fingers from his neck with alarming ease and reversed our positions. "Don't push me, Azirak." His voice still rang with the utmost calm, but the demon's enhanced senses afforded me a glimpse deeper. Heckle was not one to be fucked with. "If you wish to remain in control, you will keep Jax's end of the bargain."

"As you wish. But I will do nothing that puts myself, my clan, or the Pure in danger."

Then leave, I said with a snort. *You being here puts Sam in danger.*

The demon ignored me, calm on the outside, but on the inside, the rage was palpable. It was barely refraining itself from lunging at Heckle.

Heckle adjusted his shirt. "Now then. The task is simple. Recover the the Brim Stone and bring it to me."

"Brim Stone," Sam repeated. "Why does that sound familiar?"

"Because it's the stone that enabled Malphi to tap in to the magic of the Gray family bloodline."

"Wait." Sam's eyes grew wide. "If it's the stone Malphi had, and Malphi is dead, then who has the stone?"

Heckle pinned her with a pitying frown.

She blew a stray hair from her face and rolled her eyes. "You've gotta be shitting me…"

"I wish I were." He sighed. "I'm afraid a grievous oversight on my part allowed Malphi's stone to fall into the enemy's hands."

Sam's eyes widened, and she opened her mouth, but Azi wasn't interested in anything she had to say. Suspicion swelled and he focused on Heckle. "And what do you want with the stone?"

"As you can see," Heckle hitched a thumb over his shoulder at the carnivus. "Something is just a bit off."

He was right. Azi's memories swirled, and I knew that carnivi, like most other creatures that inhabited hell, were unable to cross to this plane. At least, not on their own. "How did it come to be here?"

"You can thank Zenak," Heckle said. He flicked a finger at the beast, frowning. "And there's plenty more where that came from. I've gotten reports from all over Harlow. Denizens of Hell have been running rampant for the last few days."

"And you believe this is Zenak's doing?" My muscles tensed, my body's natural reaction to the apprehension the demon felt. I still hadn't gotten used to it—the way my body betrayed me by reacting to the whims and desires of another. Everything was so much stronger, amplified by the demon's senses. "That my enemy has stolen the stone and is using it to call forth an army?"

"I'm afraid it is now in Zenak's possession. While one half of the stone doesn't give the demon access to all its inherit abilities, it does give a dangerous edge. It can't travel home, but it appears that it can call reinforcements."

"Wait—half?" Tendrils of worry rose from Sam's shoulders. Her pulse increased, heartbeat racing. "He doesn't have the whole thing?"

Heckle shook his head. "Sadie only had half the stone. I don't know what became of the remaining part. You'll have to find it, though. It's far too dangerous to leave it floating around."

"But if Zenak has an advantage with just half the stone, why hasn't it come for us yet?"

"It's not immediately clear what Zenak's plans are. But, knowing what we do—that it wants to destroy Azirak and take control of Sam—I believe getting to the other half of the stone before it does will benefit us all."

Azi bristled, and I felt a mix of anger and concern from the demon. "And the half of the stone that Zenak already possesses? What of that?"

"Once you retrieve the stone—*both* halves—I will dispose of them."

That wasn't going to happen. Azi had no intention of handing either half of the stone over to Heckle.

"Zenak has brought over the carnivi—and I assure you, there are more roaming the streets of Harlow. It is feasible that it has brought others as well. The tracker, perhaps?"

The shift in Azi's mood was violent. My body tensed, limbs itching to tear into something, anything. "I see," came the demon's deceptively calm response, just slightly deeper than my usual voice. "Then I suppose that escalates things."

Heckle, seemingly satisfied, gave a short nod. "In the meantime, I suggest you deal with this." He took two steps backward, melting into the darkness. A moment later, the previously frozen carnivus leaped from the shadows.

Acknowledgments

My life was a bit upside down while writing this book. My mom was diagnosed with and began treatment for stage four uterine cancer. Some of the worst days I've ever lived through happened during the construction of *Embraced*. If that sounds morbid and bleak, then let me tell you that it's anything but. Why? Because I'm still here. My mom is still here. My books, my words, are still here. And none of that would have been possible without the amazing people in my life.

Obviously my family was a huge part of that. My Aunts Nina and Lynn, and Kate—you are now and always will be a part of my family—were boundless in their support. My dad, who keeps thanking me when it is me who should be thanking him. One word. Mortimer. *mic drop* And Kevin. My husband. My rock. My reason for everything. You are the basis for every hero I write, because to me there is no one more heroic than you. When you look at me, you see someone who can do anything. Be anything. That kind of faith is the reason I am the person I am today.

To my crit partner Lynn, for your priceless feedback and

suggestion, and for all the times you checked in to see how we were doing. It might not seem like a big deal to you, but to me it was monumental. You are seven shades of awesome, girl. ;) And of course my agent, Nicole Resciniti, who I find myself in awe of. Your tireless enthusiasm and encouragement kept me from breaking some days.

To all the fantastic people at Entangled who put their time and effort into putting out amazing books. A huge thank you to Kelly Elliott for catching all those *violently* repeating words and phrases, and Heather Howland, friend and cover Goddess extraordinaire. From Ellie in publicity to my editors, the fabulous Liz Pelletier and Candace Havens, this book would be nothing more than words on a screen if you hadn't come along and helped make it pretty.

And to the readers… I might have created Jax and Sam, but you are the ones who gave them life. They would simply be names on a page without you. You're all freaking Rock Stars in my book.

And once again, to Liz, Nicole, Heather, Melanie, and Jessica, without whom this book would probably never be written. Apparently sleep is a necessary bodily function. ;)

About the Author

Jus Accardo is the author of YA paranormal romance and urban fantasy fiction. A native New Yorker, she lives in the middle of nowhere with her husband, three dogs, and sometimes guard bear, Oswald. When not writing, Jus can be found volunteering at the local animal shelter or indulging her passion for food. After being accepted to the Culinary Institute of America, she passed on the spot to pursue a career in writing and has never looked back. As far as she's concerned, she has the coolest job on earth—making stuff up for a living.

www.jusaccardo.com

Discover the **Eternal Balance** *series…*

RUINED

Jax lost the genetic lottery. Descended from Cain, the world's first murderer, he's plagued by a curse that demands violence in exchange for his happiness. Samantha can't outrun her problems. When an attack at school drives her back home, she's thrown into the path of a past—and a guy—she's been trying to forget. But someone—or something—followed her home from school: a ruthless monster with a twisted plan centuries in the making. Forced together to survive, and fighting an attraction that could destroy them both, Jax and Sam must stop a killer bent on revenge.

Also by Jus Accardo

RULES OF SURVIVAL

DENAZEN SERIES

UNTOUCHED

TOUCH

TOXIC

FACELESS

TREMBLE

www.ingramcontent.com/pod-product-compliance
Lightning Source LLC
Chambersburg PA
CBHW031951240626
47153CB00003B/942